"I requested your reassignment," Mark clarified.

In the middle of the night? Normally a transfer didn't happen instantaneously, and the idea that this one had left her feeling uncertain.

Beth's eyes narrowed. "Why would you do that?" It didn't surprise her that he had pull, but that he would use it to get her transferred did. What could be that urgent?

His eyes met hers, but there was a disconnect in them that hadn't been there earlier tonight. A sense that he saw her, but that he was no longer emotionally involved with her on a human level.

She had suddenly become a means to an end. An instrument he could use. That he could exploit.

She jerked off her mask, dropped it on the pile of rubble. "So you want to use me as bait?"

His mouth tightened. "Sweetheart, you *are* bait. I can't change that. But I fully intend to take advantage of that fact."

LORI L. HARRIS

SET UP WITH THE AGENT

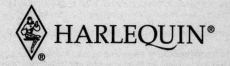

HARLEQUIN®

TORONTO • NEW YORK • LONDON
AMSTERDAM • PARIS • SYDNEY • HAMBURG
STOCKHOLM • ATHENS • TOKYO • MILAN • MADRID
PRAGUE • WARSAW • BUDAPEST • AUCKLAND

For Bobbie Laishley and Bill Laishley

And for the Harris Family: Trip, Kathy, Gracie, Mike,
Nichele, Brett, Connor, Dillon, John, Billy, Patsy and,
most of all, for Bobby. Love You All!

ISBN-13: 978-0-373-69312-2
ISBN-10:   0-373-69312-5

SET UP WITH THE AGENT

ABOUT THE AUTHOR

Lori Harris has always enjoyed competition. She grew up in southern Ohio, showing Arabian horses and Great Danes. Later she joined a shooting league where she competed head-to-head with police officers—and would be competing today if she hadn't discovered how much fun and challenging it was to write. Romantic suspense seemed a natural fit. What could be more exciting than writing about life-and-death struggles that include sexy, strong men?

When not in front of a computer, Lori enjoys remodeling her home, gardening and boating. Lori lives in Orlando, Florida, with her very own hero.

CAST OF CHARACTERS

Supervisory Special Agent Mark Gerritsen—One of the FBI's top counterterrorism agents. When the most lethal chemical weapon of all time is stolen, he'll do whatever is necessary to keep it from being used.

Special Agent Beth Benedict—In the past four months, she's survived two attempts on her life, but will she be able to survive her most recent assignment? Or the extremely handsome Mark Gerritsen?

Harvey Thesing—One of a team of chemists who developed MX141, the next generation chemical weapon. Within days of walking off with enough to take out a major city, he's dead and the chemical weapon is missing.

Special Agent Colton Larson—This competent counterterrorism agent opposes Beth's transfer to the unit.

Special Agent Jenny Springer—A nineteen-year veteran of the FBI. She understands what Beth is up against, and she believes Beth has what it takes to go the distance.

Rabbit Rheaume—When he learns Beth is working for the FBI, he locks her in the trunk of a burning car. Now he claims to know who has the stolen chemical weapon. But does he?

Leon Tyber—Who hired this shoeless hit man to take out Beth?

Supervisory Special Agent Bill Monroe—Just how far will he go to bury his own incompetence?

Prologue

FBI Special Agent Mark Gerritsen ripped his shirttails from his trousers. It was just past 3:30 a.m. on a hot July night, and he was standing on the street in front of a modest home in a quiet Frederick, Maryland, suburb.

"Has the lab determined how much of the chemical weapon is missing?" Mark kept his voice low. As he stripped off his shirt, he glanced at Special Agent Colton Larson, who stood several feet away.

Larson was also down to his T-shirt. "They're calling it sizable."

Mark offered a terse smile. "In other words they don't know, and they're trying to cover their asses."

He suspected it was also the reason the FBI hadn't been alerted of the theft until the middle of the night—because those in charge of security, of protecting the people from the kind of occurrence that had just taken place, had been scrambling to protect their jobs instead of the American public.

Leaving his shirt hanging over the open car door, Mark grabbed the heavy body armor off the seat and settled it over his shoulders. He shrugged the protection into position before pressing down on the Velcro straps. The rest of the counterterrorism unit had been contacted but was unlikely to arrive in time, which meant Mark and Larson would be working with a local SWAT team.

The target was a home two doors down from their current location. Mark scanned the front of the residence. Except for the dim front porch light, the small, brick ranch house with peeling trim paint had been dark when they'd arrived and remained that way.

The owner, Dr. Harvey Thesing, made a good wage, but from the brief background information Mark had obtained en route, over the past year Thesing had been spending his money on environmental causes. Which should have tipped off his superiors that no matter what his credentials were, Thesing wasn't the best chemist to work on MX141.

Along with the rundown on Thesing, Mark had also received one on the chemical weapon. Though fairly stable in the powdered form, once dissolved in a liquid and vaporized, its lethal power was immeasurable.

Bottom line, they were talking some nasty stuff.

Mark checked out the surrounding residences. "How are those evacuations coming?" While he had been meeting with the SWAT guys, Larson had been seeing to the perimeter.

Larson looked up. "Local cops have cleared a block in all directions and are in the process of closing off roads."

Mark would have liked to ask for a larger area, but there just wasn't time for that luxury right now. It was a decision that he hoped he didn't end up regretting. "Make sure they stick close by in case we need to get more people out."

A SWAT team member rounded the front end of Mark's car, striding soundlessly toward them. "Car's in the garage. Bedrooms appear to be at the back."

Mark grabbed the olive drab hazmat suit and stepped

into it. Because he'd been assimilating a lot of information when they'd met five minutes ago, it took him a second to recall the officer's name. Rogers?

Mark slid his arms into the sleeves of the suit. "But you don't know which one Thesing is using? Or if he's even in that area of the house."

"No. We're not picking up any sounds inside."

Which meant they might find an empty house. That Thesing could already be putting his plan into motion.

Mark zipped up the lightweight suit. But what was Thesing's agenda? What in the hell did a tree hugger do with a chemical weapon that he'd been instrumental in developing?

"What about a basement?" Mark asked.

"There's one."

"Any type of entrance?"

"Two well windows that are boarded up from inside."

Was it possible that Thesing was sleeping down there? Perhaps because with the recent heat wave it was cooler?

Mark grabbed his holstered weapon and strapped it on. "Any word on whether Thesing owns a gun?"

"Nothing registered."

Which, given current gun laws, didn't mean a whole hell of a lot. Thesing could be sitting on a whole arsenal.

Rogers scanned the area quickly and then returned his attention to Mark. "How do you want to do this?"

"Covert entry through the front door. I'll need for one of your men to handle the pick gun, then hang around long enough to offer some initial cover. Once Larson and I are in, though, your man needs to back off immediately. Best-case scenario, we reach the chemist before he has time to get to the stuff."

Mark looked up, his gaze connecting with Rogers's. "No one goes in without full hazmat gear, understand?" He waited until the officer nodded before continuing. "Have the rest of your men keep the windows and doors under hard surveillance, while still maintaining a safe distance."

"Does this stuff have a name?" Rogers asked.

Larson had just stepped past Mark to grab a hazmat suit. "Yeah. Scary."

Even as Rogers offered a tight nod and turned away, Mark sensed the local cop's frustration at being asked to respond to a situation where critical information was being withheld.

Not that Mark had any choice in the matter.

They were under orders to avoid full disclosure of MX141's capabilities, something that made him extremely uncomfortable. But if everything went well in the next few minutes, if the MX141 was recovered without incident, the decision to withhold certain facts could turn out to be the right one.

At least, that's what he was hoping.

Grabbing the twelve-gauge he'd left on the sedan's floorboard, Mark spilled the box of shotgun shells onto the floor mat. After collecting six of them, he backed out of Larson's way and then waited while the other man did the same. They'd worked together often enough that there was no need for discussion.

With his chest already beginning to tighten with tension, Mark glanced across the hood of the Taurus and toward the residence. Still no sign of life. Maybe he should at least be thankful for that.

Mark took the lead, and by the time they reached the front door, a SWAT officer was already in place. Mark and Larson tugged down their night-vision goggles and adjusted their breathing apparatuses before lowering their hazmat hoods into place.

At Mark's nod, the officer inserted the pick gun into the first of two locks. In seconds the door was unlocked, but it took another few to dispense with the safety chain.

As the SWAT officer stepped out of the way, Mark moved inside, intent on reaching the bedroom hallway as quickly and as soundlessly as possible.

The door to the first bedroom was open. A home office. Unoccupied. The doors to the other two remained closed. Mark stopped next to the nearest of them, and then waited for Larson to reach the other one.

At Mark's signal, both men checked to see if their door was unlocked. Larson offered a slight nod, indicating that his was. Mark did the same. On Mark's next signal they entered their assigned rooms as silently as possible, twelve-gauge shotguns leading the way.

Mark did a quick sweep before focusing on the double bed covered in unfolded clothes. He made sure Thesing wasn't buried beneath the laundry, and then did a fast inspection of the closet. He hooked up with Larson in the hallway again.

Taking the point position, Mark moved cautiously toward the living areas. The element of surprise was off the table now. If Thesing was in the house, even if he was in the basement, it was unlikely that he'd still be unaware of their presence. Which made it more likely they'd be facing an armed suspect.

Motioning Larson to hang back, Mark skirted the dining room table. Cardboard moving boxes sealed with tape surrounded the table, and a mountain of newspapers covered it.

Because of the hazmat gear, Mark was drowning in

sweat, but his breathing was still slow and easy. Like the bedroom he'd just left, the kitchen was a mess. Trash overflowed the fifty-five-gallon waste can in the center of the room, and a healthy roach population was chowing down on the food remnants covering pots and pans and plates. For a man worried about the environment, it looked as if he was well on the way to creating his very own toxic-waste site.

The family room was just beyond and appeared to be in the same condition as the rest of the house.

Backtracking, Mark returned to the kitchen where he waited for Larson to get into position before opening what Mark had correctly assumed would be the door to the basement.

Positioned just to the left of the opening, he peered into the lower level, looking for any hint of movement. Seeing none, he slowly lowered his foot onto the first tread, allowing the wood to absorb his weight.

As he continued to work his way down the stairs, his breathing became less smooth, less even. He kept his back pressed to the wall. Larson was covering him from the head of the stairs, but Mark was still in a very exposed position.

Halfway down, a single tread gave under his weight, the resulting sharp squeal enough to wake anyone. Seeing it as his only option, Mark took the remaining steps quickly and noisily. At the bottom, he dropped into a crouch next to the wall.

The conditions in the basement were even worse than those above stairs. Along with stacks of junk, there were more piles of newspapers and cardboard boxes and bags of trash. Why in the hell would Thesing hoard garbage? What kind of nut case were they dealing with here?

Larson had made it to the bottom of the steps and spread out slightly to Mark's left as both men moved forward cautiously.

A workbench stretched along the closest wall and was the only relatively neat area. A washer and dryer occupied the opposite wall. In between was a gauntlet of every type of imaginable junk—a tricycle, a dollhouse, an old sewing machine. A rolling cabinet for tools. More sealed plastic bags.

It wasn't until Mark got past them that he saw the bed tucked back in the far corner. And Harvey Thesing's body on the floor next to it. Even from his current position, Mark was fairly certain the chemist was dead, but kept his weapon leveled on him as he closed the distance.

It looked as if a shotgun had been used, the blast to Thesing's midsection nearly cutting him in two, while the one to his head had taken off half his skull.

Knowing it was a waste of time, he checked for a pulse and found none. But as he started to pull his hand away, he realized that, given the cool conditions of the basement the body was warmer than he would have anticipated. He checked the facial muscles—the first place that any signs of rigor mortis would appear—but found no rigidity.

"How long?" Larson asked.

"If I had to make a guess?" Using the method to determine time of death was risky at best. "I'd say only a short time—possibly less than an hour."

Mark desperately wanted to plow his fist into something—into anything. If the damn lab hadn't been trying to cover their asses… If they'd made the call an hour earlier…

Talk about being screwed. Even the relatively short lead

time wasn't going to help them. For the moment at least, they were chasing a ghost.

A ghost armed with the most lethal chemical weapon ever developed.

Chapter One

Four Months Later

Leaving her dark, wool coat and white scarf draped across the chair, FBI Special Agent Beth Benedict paced to the bookcase and scanned the titles. *Experimental Psychology, Evaluation of Sexual Disorders, The Problem of Maladaptive Behavior*—a bevy of volumes detailing human psychoses. Exactly what she would expect to find on a psychologist's shelf.

As with her previous two sessions, she was the last patient of the day. The receptionist had shown her into Dr. Carmichael's office, indicating that she should take a seat in one of the high-backed contemporary chairs. Dr. Carmichael would be with her shortly.

But since Beth had been released from the hospital, she'd found it very difficult to sit still for any length of time. Another reason that she needed to be out in the field and not trapped behind a desk.

She took a deep breath in preparation for the coming confrontation. The FBI had trained her how to deceive criminals, how to gain their trust, so scamming one psychologist shouldn't be all that hard. She just needed to stick with the plan, with her "blueprint of progress."

This week she'd remain calm and in control, no tears, no outbursts. And no more stony silences that suggested she was bucking authority. By her next appointment, the claustrophobia issue would be nearly resolved.

As with any type of deception, the key was to keep it believable.

When she heard the office door open behind her, her shoulder muscles tightened, and the headache that she'd been coping with exploded at the base of her skull.

Dr. Samuel Carmichael paused momentarily in the opening. He was somewhere in his late forties, with thick, prematurely gray hair and a quick smile. Because any good con required that you know your mark, she'd done her homework. He liked to sail and was on his second marriage, this one to a law student half his age.

"Sorry about running late," the psychologist offered as he pushed the door closed.

"No problem." Beth took a seat and settled back, giving the illusion that she was comfortable.

"Can I get you some water before we get started?"

"No. Thanks."

Taking the chair opposite hers, Carmichael propped his right ankle atop his left knee before resting the legal pad in his lap. "So how do you think you're doing?"

"Actually, a little better."

"What about the nightmares? Are you still experiencing them?"

"Occasionally." She kept the confident and somewhat bland smile on her face. Though this was only her third session, she knew the routine, so she waited for the psychologist to pursue the current subject.

"Are you saying there's been a decrease in their frequency?"

"Yes. Some." In reality, the opposite was true. Every time she was lucky enough to fall asleep, it was only a matter of time before she sat straight up, her heart pounding, the scent of spilled gasoline so real that it usually took her several seconds to realize that the smell was a remembered one, a cruel joke played by her own mind.

Dr. Carmichael scribbled a note. "And when they do occur, would you characterize them as any less vivid than when we started meeting?"

"Definitely." She knew she needed to start offering more than short responses, but despite her earlier resolve, she was finding it surprisingly difficult, her emotions already bubbling to the surface. Her palms were now damp and as she met Carmichael's gaze, her respiration quickened, almost as if he had leveled a gun at her chest.

But in some ways, the situation she found herself in now was just as much a life-or-death struggle as the event that had landed her here. Dr. Samuel Carmichael held her career in his hands. And since her career was her life….

Carmichael leaned back in his chair. "What about the claustrophobia?"

"It's better." Another short response. "I'm back to riding elevators. Wouldn't you say that's a pretty major step?"

She managed a slight smile, but when she tried to force it a bit wider, she felt her facial muscles freeze. And knew that she'd made a mistake. She could see it in his washed-out blue eyes and in the way his mouth tightened.

"Beth." Carmichael uncrossed his legs. "I've been in

practice for a lot of years. I know when I'm being manipulated. I can't help you unless you're open with me."

She kept her gaze level. How should she respond? Pretend confusion? Try a small amount of honesty?

Taking a deep breath, she let it out slowly, having decided the latter was going to be the best course of action.

"You're right. But you have to understand what I need to get better. I need work. Real work. I've been pulled out of the field and assigned to administrative duties. Do you have any idea what that includes? I run a copier. I collate reports for other agents. I answer the phone."

"You do recognize that your boss, that Bill Monroe is concerned that the incident has left you—"

Irritation kicked in. "Incident? Isn't that a slightly benign description for being locked in the trunk of a burning car? The fact that I have some difficulty sleeping, that I've had occasional problems handling tight spaces isn't all that unusual, is it, given the circumstances?"

"No. What you're feeling is quite normal." Holding a pencil in one hand, he ran the fingers of the other one up and down the length as he studied her. "So you believe that you should be put back out into the field? Where your failure to function at a crucial moment could possibly endanger your life or the life of an innocent bystander or coworker?"

She held on to her irritation. "I recognize that I do have issues at the moment, but I believe they are temporary and controllable. I don't feel they undermine my ability to do my job."

"So, if you don't believe you need help, why are you here?" He paused before adding, "My understanding is that these sessions are voluntary."

"That is what the manual says," she agreed. Unable to sit still any longer, she got up and paced to the window. Even though her SAC—Special Agent in Charge—had characterized the counseling as voluntary, she knew better.

"Don't you want to improve?"

"Sure." And she wanted to keep her job, too. She looked out at the dark night. The window overlooked the parking garage across the street where she'd left her car.

"Of course I want to get better." She just couldn't see how dwelling on problems could be therapeutic. That wasn't the way she'd been raised. You get knocked down, you get back up. End of story.

With her carefully constructed blueprint of progress a bust, she decided maybe it was the right time to put at least a few cards on the table. And at the same time momentarily steer the conversation away from her. "You attended University of Maryland, didn't you?"

"That's right."

She faced him. "And graduated the same year as Bill Monroe?"

It was Carmichael's turn to look uncomfortable. "So you think you're being set up in some way? That I'm your boss's hit man?"

"It crossed my mind." Having given up all attempts to control her body language, she tightened her arms in front of her. "I suppose after that remark, you'll be adding paranoia to the list."

Carmichael's eyes narrowed and his lips thinned. "Do you consider yourself to be overly suspicious of the motives of people around you?"

She pretended to consider the possibility. When she'd been doing the background check on Carmichael, she'd done a little self-diagnosing while she was at it. She might be experiencing a sense of fatalism where her job was concerned, but it was fully grounded in cold, hard facts.

Beth realized the psychologist was still waiting for an answer on the paranoia issue. "No. I don't consider myself to be paranoid."

Even if Carmichael didn't know the real reason she was undergoing counseling, the only reason she still had a job, she did. She was the prosecution's only witness on the Rabbit Rheaume money laundering case, and they were worried that she'd fall apart during cross examination. These sessions were meant to keep her functioning until after the trial—until after she'd taken the stand and the feds had their conviction.

But once they did, all bets would be off.

For more than two years now, since she'd gone over his head, Bill Monroe had been looking for a way to get rid of her—not an easy task considering the previous glowing evaluations he'd given her.

The knot in her gut tightened. Even before she'd gone in undercover, landing a position as Rabbit Rheaume's assistant, she'd been trying to hold on, to play Monroe's game. She was hoping that those above him would somehow miraculously recognize that he was conducting a witch hunt against her. But even from the beginning she'd known that her survival was unlikely. That even though she'd managed to survive Rabbit's car trunk, it was unlikely she'd survive Monroe. He was a twenty-two-year veteran of the Bureau. Part of the men's club. And the FBI historically tended to protect those in higher positions, sacrificing lower-ranked employees.

Realizing Carmichael was watching her again, she

slammed the door closed on that line of thought. She couldn't afford it right now. "Maybe I'm a little lost at the moment, that's all."

"We all are sometimes. But none of us has to remain that way." Carmichael crossed to his desk, opened the top drawer and pulled out a prescription pad.

She found it difficult to hide her exasperation. What kind of pill would it be this time? She'd tried taking what he'd prescribed on the first visit, something for anxiety, but when the drug had interfered with her ability to function, she'd quit taking it. She'd needed to stay clear-headed, keep her wits about her.

When he finished writing, he ripped off the top sheet and handed it to her. Even though she had no intention of having the prescription filled, Beth glanced down at the writing. The name Harriet Thompson was followed by a local phone number.

"She's a colleague of mine. She didn't attend Maryland and doesn't know Bill Monroe."

Her eyes narrowed briefly as she wondered if she was in fact paranoid.

"You're a very strong woman, Beth, but you still need to talk to someone."

She glanced up. "Are you firing me?"

"No. I just want to be sure that the next time we meet, you're here for the right reasons. I can help you, but only if you let me."

ONLY MINUTES LATER Beth buttoned the heavy, wool coat over her navy-blue suit and pulled on gloves before pushing open the office building's exterior door and stepping out into the cold night. As the early-November wind cut through her, Carmichael's words lingered in the back of her mind.

She'd always considered herself to be tough and competent. During the sixteen weeks at Quantico, she'd physically and mentally outperformed most of her class, even those with military or law enforcement backgrounds.

But in a single night, that had all changed. She'd gone from tough to frightened. And now, nearly four months after she'd escaped the trunk of a burning car, she still felt trapped, as if everything around her was going up in flames. Her career. Her relationship with her father.

She couldn't afford to look weak, though. Not if she wanted to keep her job. And not when she took the stand at the Rheaume trial. If the prosecution lost there, getting a conviction on the connected attempted-murder charge was going to become even tougher. How was she going to live with herself if the man who had tried to kill her wasn't made to pay?

She crossed the now-deserted street. Though it was just past seven-thirty, there were few lights on in the surrounding buildings. Which wasn't surprising since most of them were private medical offices.

Her footsteps rang out sharply. The little bit of snow they'd had earlier had melted, but now with nightfall, the moisture had refrozen, creating an extremely thin shield of ice. Not enough to make driving dangerous, but enough to make walking a little trickier, especially in pumps.

She headed into the parking garage. During normal business hours there was an attendant at the entrance, but the enclosure was now deserted.

As she stepped around the barrier bar, a red Beemer came down the ramp, headed for the exit. Out of habit, she reached inside her jacket to check her weapon, but then remembered she'd locked it in her trunk.

Seeing the woman behind the wheel, Beth relaxed. For the past few months, she'd done a lot of looking over her shoulder, waiting to see if Rheaume would try to stack the deck in his favor. It was just another reason that she was constantly on edge, and why she refused to take the anti-anxiety medication. And the reason she'd be armed at her next appointment despite Carmichael's office policy. There was a difference between paranoia and vigilance.

As she passed the elevator doors, she glanced at them but didn't slow. She'd managed to ride up in the one at the office two days ago, but at the moment she didn't feel like trying it again.

If the outside temperature had seemed frigid, inside the garage was even worse. She slid her gloved hands into her pockets. A few cars—a green Taurus, a blue Explorer and a white Escalade were clustered near the entrance—but the rest of the lower level had cleared out. Unfortunately, it had been full when she'd arrived, so she'd been forced to leave her car on the second level. She hiked up the ramp.

Several of the fluorescent lights overhead were out. As quickly as she looked up, she diverted her gaze from the reinforced-concrete ceiling. For some reason even in this reasonably wide-open space, she felt as if all that weight was pressing down on her, as if she'd be buried beneath it. Inhaling sharply, she forced her hands a little deeper into her pockets.

She was fine. Absolutely fine. The claustrophobia was getting better. Maybe it was resolving more slowly than she wanted, but she just needed to keep pushing herself.

Reaching the top of the incline, she spotted her red

Taurus off to the right, but instead of walking toward it, she stopped in her tracks. A white Chevy van with heavily tinted windows had been backed in next to the Taurus. Her fingers closed around the car keys in her pocket. There had been a maroon Honda in the slot earlier and quite a few empty spaces near the elevator.

She scanned the rest of the second level and, finding it deserted, studied the van again. Something just didn't feel right. With this level pretty much empty, why would the driver choose to park there? And more important, why go to the trouble of backing in?

The front seats were empty, but that didn't eliminate the possibility that someone was in the backend, waiting to roll open the side door, waiting to pull her inside when she tried to reach the driver's door of her car.

Should she bail?

And do what, though? Use her cell phone to call a cop? What if she was wrong about the van? What if in this one instance she actually had taken that downhill slide from cautious to paranoid?

If so, calling Baltimore PD would have been a bad idea. Once the cops realized she was a fed, there was very little chance it wouldn't get back to Monroe. Or that he wouldn't use it against her, claiming that the incident further demonstrated her inability to do her job.

She took a deep breath and let it out slowly. *Think.* No one had followed her here. She was certain of that. And for the past few months she'd been careful to avoid any hint of a pattern in her activities—she never took the same route, never scheduled an appointment on the same day. But all three of her sessions with Carmichael had come at the end of the day…

And then she realized if Rheaume had sent someone after her, bailing now wouldn't stop them. There would be a next time. One she might not see coming until it was too late.

Better to confront it now.

As a blast of frigid air screamed through the garage, she strode purposefully toward her car, a plan already formulated. She wasn't going to let them win—not the Monroes or the Carmichaels, and definitely not the Rabbit Rheaumes.

Keeping her eyes on the van, her thumb worked the automatic trunk release on the key fob. If anyone was in the van, they obviously were waiting until she walked between the two vehicles. Otherwise they would have already made their move.

The raised trunk would offer some protection while she grabbed her weapon. And if she was wrong, if the van was empty, she'd just get in her car and go home. Soak in a hot bath. Forget she'd nearly made a fool of herself.

She was already leaning into the trunk when she heard the nearly silent footsteps behind her. Her fingers closed around the holstered SIG-Sauer, and she had it free of leather when the sharp pop echoed. White-hot heat streaked just above her right temple.

Diving toward the side of the car, hoping to use it as cover, she brought the SIG-Sauer up, getting her first look at the shooter—a stocky male in dark clothing. She fired two quick rounds. Both slammed into his chest.

He kept coming.

A loud crack sounded. The taillight next to her shattered. Small bits of plastic exploded, some of it hitting her in the face, causing her to blink. Causing her third shot to miss.

As a bullet punctured the fender next to her, she squeezed the trigger again, this time going for a head shot.

Like a tethered pit bull hitting the end of its chain, the guy's forward momentum vanished, and for the briefest of moments it was as if both time and motion stood still. His expression changed, bloomed from one of aggression to chagrin and then to stunned disbelief.

And then time kicked in again, and he was flying backward.

Chapter Two

Beth got to her feet, her weapon trained on her attacker as she checked out the darkened garage for additional signs of danger.

Nothing.

No hint of movement or sound. But then, she hadn't heard her attacker until it was nearly too late. Where had he come from? Why hadn't she seen him sooner?

Her pulse scrambled uncontrollably. No matter how fast her lungs worked, she remained winded, gasping for air.

Keeping her weapon leveled at the body on the ground fifteen feet away, she forced herself to focus.

Part of her training had involved role-playing, learning how to survive a situation like the one she'd just been involved in, one where taking the time to weigh options could get you killed. And it was that same training she fell back on now, her attention flipping between her attacker and her surroundings.

She kicked aside the weapon he'd dropped—a .45 Smith & Wesson automatic—before closing the last few feet and getting the first clear look at his injuries. His right eye was gone.

As she reached down to check for a pulse—something she knew was a wasted action even before she did it—the warm scent of fresh blood reached up and grabbed her. Swallowing the bile that piled in her throat, she straightened.

He was younger than she'd first thought, midtwenties maybe. He wore a black ski cap pulled low over his ears. Seeing no sign of hair, she assumed his head was clean shaven. The rest of his clothing—jeans and sweatshirt—were also black.

When her gaze made it as far as his feet, she realized the reason she hadn't heard him. He wasn't wearing shoes. Who goes barefoot in November? In freezing temperatures?

Still facing him, she backed away, fumbling for the cell phone at her waist. She couldn't stop her hand from shaking, so it took several tries to disengage the phone from the clip.

After placing calls to 911 and to Bill Monroe, she sat on the bumper of her car to wait. It was unlikely that Monroe would show up. When she'd reached him, he'd been at some type of social function.

For the first time, she allowed herself to really think about what had just taken place. She'd taken a life. And no matter how prepared she'd thought she was to do it, how certain she'd been that she could live with it, she suddenly realized she might have been wrong.

Inhaling sharply, she tried to dislodge the growing tightness in her chest. She couldn't fall apart now. Deep breaths. Cleansing breaths. She'd killed a man, and there was no going back.

An hour later Beth was still sitting on the bumper of her car, but she was no longer alone. Minutes after she'd placed the 911 call, the first responding officer—a street cop—had secured the area and taken down an initial report.

Two Baltimore detectives and the crime-scene unit were the next to arrive. And less than two minutes ago, three FBI special agents from the Baltimore office had shown up. At one time she'd considered them office allies. But ever since Monroe had tagged her for termination, they'd distanced themselves from her.

It was always the office relationships that were the first to go. Next would come the stripping of security clearances. So far she'd dodged that bullet, for the same reason she still had a job—because they needed her testimony. Testimony that would carry more weight coming from a special agent whose security clearance hadn't been downgraded or revoked.

She lowered the wad of fast-food napkins she'd found in her glove box and had been pressing to the side of her head. The gash just above her right temple was a minor one, but like most head wounds, it had bled pretty profusely at first. She glanced down at her shoulder. The white silk scarf was probably a lost cause, but because the coat she wore was navy-blue wool, the bloodstain wasn't particularly noticeable and would probably clean up okay.

Her gaze returned to the three special agents and two detectives who were still conversing near the ramp. What were they discussing now? Just the shooting? Or were her coworkers eagerly explaining to the detectives that her appointment tonight had been with a shrink and not some other type of doctor?

Beth shifted her attention away from them and onto the dead man. His body remained uncovered. At least the shooter had a name now. Leon Tyber. The shoeless hit man. But even if he'd forgotten footwear, he'd remembered to wear body armor, the reason the first two shots to his chest hadn't stopped him.

He'd come prepared to take me down swiftly and efficiently. But instead, I killed him.

As another sharp breeze blew through the structure, she shivered. She wasn't really dressed to hang out in a cold garage. Like everyone else at the scene, she was waiting for the medical examiner to show up and release the body for transport to the morgue. Until he did, she couldn't move her car without destroying evidence. Of course, if she'd been really eager to go home, she could have called a cab and come back tomorrow to pick up her car.

Hearing footsteps, she glanced up. Special Agent Tom Weston, a seventeen-year FBI veteran, walked over and propped his backside next to hers. He was tall, well built. In her early days in Baltimore, he'd been somewhat of a mentor to her. Up until a year ago, she'd considered him a friend.

Hands clasped in front of him, he looked over at her and then motioned at her injured head. "Maybe you should consider a trip to the emergency room to get that checked out."

"It's just a crease. I'm fine."

"What you are," Tom said, "is lucky."

Frowning, she refolded the napkins and rested them against her scalp again, trying to ignore the now throbbing headache. Tom's comment didn't surprise her. It did however sting more than she would have expected. "What I am is good at my job."

"I didn't mean to suggest—"

Her eyes narrowed. "Of course you didn't." But they both knew better. Recently her accomplishments and skills had increasingly been downplayed. "And the fact that I'm not included in the Friday-night get-togethers doesn't mean a damn thing, either."

Beth knew she was venturing into areas that would only serve to further damage her relationship with Weston, a man she had once held in great respect.

"You're shutting me out," she said, and glanced down, not wanting to meet his eyes, not wanting him to see how much his actions had hurt her. "I didn't expect that." She looked over at him. "I actually thought you would be the only one in the office willing to back me up."

"Damn it, Beth." Tom grimaced. "I have two kids already in college and another one starting next year. I'm not about to put my job in jeopardy."

"There's a name for that, Tom. Careerism. The practice of protecting one's career. At the cost of one's integrity."

When Tom shifted his gaze to the group of men near the ramp, Beth sensed he was looking for a reason to leave her, to rejoin the others. And at the same time she realized even if he'd been going about it very cautiously, he had been trying to be somewhat supportive. At least for tonight.

"I'm sorry, Tom. I'm not being completely fair here."

He rubbed his face, suddenly looking even more exhausted than when he'd sat. "You have nothing to apologize for." He studied her, a deep furrow between his brows. "But why didn't you come to me before going over Monroe's head?"

She balled up the bloody napkins. "Like you said, you have kids in college. I don't."

"But you had to know that you were risking your career. That Monroe wouldn't hesitate to blow you away if you said anything about his screw-up."

"He didn't give me a choice." Even she heard the edge of anger in her voice. "It was a viable lead, and he didn't assign it. And because he didn't, terrorism got another payday." Beth realized the other men were watching them now, and lowered her voice. "I took an oath to protect and defend this country," she said. "Not keep my mouth shut."

Tom nudged her shoulder with his. "You always were a damned idealist."

"So were you," she offered with a sad smile.

He nodded. "Back when I could afford to be."

"What did Monroe have to say when he called you tonight?"

"Just that I was to head up the investigation and he'd talk to you in the morning. There's nothing for you to worry about. It was obviously self-defense."

He glanced toward where the other men were still talking. This time she didn't think it was because he was looking to escape her. But then his facial expression suddenly changed, went from one of fatigue to near anger. "What in the hell is Mark Gerritsen doing here?"

Surprised to hear the name, Beth followed Tom's gaze, certain he must be mistaken. Unfortunately, he wasn't. At six-three and deadly handsome, Special Agent Gerritsen was easy to recognize even from where she sat. Currently he was talking with the other two FBI special agents and the two detectives.

She frowned. Why would the FBI's leading counterterrorism specialist have any interest in what had taken place here tonight? In a simple shooting?

Mark suddenly broke away from the other men and walked toward Tom and Beth. When he reached the dead shooter, he stopped to examine the body.

Beneath the beige trench coat, Mark Gerritsen wore a dark suit. The collar of his white oxford-cloth shirt was open, and his hair looked as if he'd plowed his fingers through it more than once.

Not so amazingly, as she watched the FBI's best-of-the-best straighten and walk toward them, her thoughts had nothing to do with national security, and everything to do with the last time they'd met. A meeting where she had come off as completely foolish and sophomoric. A meeting she was hoping he didn't recall.

But it probably hadn't been all that memorable for him. During her sixteen weeks of new recruit training, he'd been her counterterrorism instructor. There hadn't been a female in the class who hadn't been in lust with Mark Gerritsen, her included. After all, when it came to aphrodisiacs, power coupled with intellect, looks and honor was damn potent.

Back then he'd been newly divorced and had a couple of kids. Was that still the case?

Tom had stood as soon as he'd seen Gerritsen, but she waited until he reached them to get to her feet.

Tom held out his hand, his expression anything but welcoming. "Gerritsen, let me introduce—"

Mark's gaze connected with Tom's briefly before immediately shifting to Beth. "We've actually met."

It was only when he extended his hand to her that she realized she still held the bloody napkins. After quickly shoving the wad into her pocket, she shook his hand, lifting her gaze to his face at the same time.

His eyes were brown, and at the moment the brows were drawn down tight over them. There was a rawness to his features—eyes that were deep set, a nose that wasn't quite straight, a mouth that rarely smiled. But when it did, there was a dimple just to the left of it. She'd seen it on only one occasion—the one she was hoping he'd forgotten.

"I hear you had a rough night," Mark said.

"Oh, I don't know." She tried for a confident tone. "All in all, I'd say mine was better than Leon Tyber's."

Mark's lips shifted toward a smile, but it never actually appeared. He now glanced over his shoulder at the body, too. "At what point did you discover he was wearing body armor?"

"When my first two shots didn't stop him." If he was impressed, it didn't show.

"How many rounds total?" He seemed to be studying her a little too intently, and she again wondered what his interest could be in the shooting. She couldn't imagine Tyber having any connection to terrorism.

"He got off three, I fired four." She was aware that Tom still stood beside her and that there was some animosity between the two men. She wondered about its origin.

"And you think Rheaume hired him?" Mark asked.

She paused. How would he have known that? Then she realized the other agents had undoubtedly filled him in. What else had they said? "It went down like a hit." She took half a step backward. Somehow it suddenly felt as if he'd invaded her space. "Not to mention the fact that street punks don't usually carry twelve-hundred-dollar weapons and wear body armor."

"What makes you so certain it isn't linked to another case?"

"Because the Rheaume case is the only one I'm involved with." She wasn't about to elaborate on the reason that it was her only one. If he didn't already know about her current employment problems—something she figured was fairly unlikely since that kind of thing tended to get around the Bureau pretty quickly—she saw no reason to enlighten him. To make herself look worse in his eyes.

"What brings you here?" Tom asked.

Mark's mouth tightened. "Perhaps you could excuse us, Tom. I need to speak with Beth."

Those words took her by surprise. Especially since she'd assumed he was there to see one of the other agents or even Tom. What would Mark Gerritsen need to discuss with her that he wouldn't want to talk about in front of Tom Weston?

Tom glanced at her. "Are you okay here?"

What was he asking? Why did he seem so hesitant to leave her with Mark? Was it concern for her? Or was he simply worried she'd do something to make their boss look bad? And that as the senior special agent at the scene, he would somehow be held responsible?

"I'm fine." Those two words were quickly becoming her new mantra.

Mark waited to speak until after Tom walked off. "*Fine* might be an overstatement. If you haven't already had someone look at your head, maybe you should."

"Thanks for the concern, but I'm okay. And I'm curious about what would bring you here tonight."

Mark turned his back to the breeze. "I just came from trying to see a friend of yours."

Hands shoved deep into the pockets of her coat, she leaned against the car fender, even more perplexed. "What friend?"

"Rabbit Rheaume."

The name took her by surprise. "Really?" Glancing down, noticing the ripped-out knee on her pantyhose, she immediately lifted her gaze again. She wanted to look more confident, more together than she felt. "I plan to pay him a visit tomorrow. To give him the good news about Leon Tyber."

Mark stared at her. "You'll find him at the morgue."

Chapter Three

Mark followed Beth into her small bungalow. It hadn't taken much to convince her to let him bring her home. Or to control the conversation during the drive. They'd covered the recent weather and a number of other unmemorable topics. And the only time she'd brought up Rheaume's death, he'd suggested they wait until they reached her place. Her agreement had come in the form of silence.

Just inside the door, she stopped to disarm the security system and to turn on the foyer and living room lights, but then kept moving. "Make yourself comfortable. I'm going to put on some coffee."

"Sure."

As she walked on through to what he assumed was the kitchen, he didn't follow. He wanted to give her some space. Even if she wasn't displaying any of the obvious signs of distress, she was still coping with it internally. He recalled the first time he'd used lethal force, the way his hands had shaken for hours afterward. How, for nearly a week following the incident, even when he hadn't been thinking about the shooting, his hands would suddenly start to tremble again.

Turning, he checked out the living room. Though the house and neighborhood dated before the 1940s, the inside of the home had been decorated with an almost loftlike starkness. Lots of metal and wood and bright colors.

He glanced at the red chair and hassock in front of the unlit fireplace and found himself wishing he could afford the luxury of just sitting, of sharing a cup of coffee with a woman without having to interrogate her.

Unfortunately he couldn't do either of those things. He had a meeting in Boston in the morning, and in the meantime he had a job to do.

The kitchen light went on and then there was an extended stretch of silence where he was left to wonder what she was doing.

After several minutes, he finally took half a step toward the kitchen. "Can I help?"

"No," she answered in a voice that was an octave higher than usual. "That's okay. I've got it."

"How long have you lived here?"

"Three years," she said over the soft thump of a cabinet door closing. "I bought it as soon as I was assigned to the Baltimore office."

Hearing the kitchen faucet run and figuring that she'd be busy for a few minutes more at least, he stepped across the foyer and into the darkened home office. At one time the space would have been a formal dining room. Like the living room, the furnishings were also contemporary. He took off the khaki-colored trench coat and folded it over the back of the desk chair, before turning his attention to the wall of family photos.

She was the only daughter of a diplomat. Geoffrey Benedict had done stints in both France and Turkey, which accounted for Beth's proficiency in Turkish and French. And for the numerous black-and-white photos with European and Middle-Eastern backgrounds.

Though she held a degree in accounting, he suspected the FBI had been more impressed with her language skills. Since becoming a government employee, she'd added Farsi and Spanish to the list. And with the global environment out there now, that ability would only become more important as time went on.

So why was Bill Monroe so determined to terminate her? Was she really the loose gun her personnel file suggested? Unwilling to follow orders? Unable to function as part of a team? That wasn't the recruit Mark remembered.

He'd first noticed her in his class because, even at twenty-three, she'd been a standout. Not only physically but also intellectually. Her questions had demonstrated an awareness of world views that most of the other recruits had yet to recognize. She had intrigued him then. And she intrigued him now. Perhaps more than was wise.

Suddenly the overhead light went on. "Make yourself at home."

Glancing over his shoulder, he didn't miss the slight rebuff. Or that she'd taken off the coat and scarf, but didn't appear to have checked the head wound. If she had, she would have wiped away the dried blood on the side of her neck. She had dark-gray eyes and nearly black hair that was on the short side. And if anything, she was more attractive than she'd been three years ago.

"Coffee will be a few minutes," she offered as she took an additional step into the room. "Maybe while we're waiting on it, you could tell me what this is about. Why you went to see Rheaume? And why you came to see me?"

He turned and faced her. "What I'm about to say can't leave this room." He held her gaze. "You understand?"

"Okay." She crossed to the desk chair and sat, looking up at him, her hands resting palm up in her lap. She wanted to look at ease, but he sensed she wasn't.

Maybe he was making a mistake here. Several members of the task force, men he trusted, had questioned the advisability of approaching Beth Benedict. But given the situation, he didn't feel he could ignore any lead.

"Nearly four months ago, despite tight security, a canister of MX141 was taken by Harvey Thesing, a chemist who had been instrumental in its development. He not only managed to circumvent the stringent safeguards that were in place, he was also able to conceal the theft for several days."

"And what exactly is MX141?"

"The next generation chemical weapon. So deadly that exposure to the vaporized form kills in less than a minute. With other types of exposure, either to the skin or ingestion, you're looking at five minutes tops."

He grabbed the remaining chair. It didn't surprise him that she didn't know anything about MX141. Currently, because there was a very real concern of a full-scale panic should the public learn about the theft, only key members of the administration, the defense department and Mark's unit knew anything about it.

"By the time the theft was noticed, Thesing was dead and the container was missing. The assumption at the time was that the weapon had changed hands, and Thesing's buyer had decided it was cheaper to pay with a bullet than with cash."

"I'm assuming his bank account supported the theory."

He nodded. "No unusual activity."

She shifted her hands in her lap, the motion drawing his gaze down. She'd removed her damaged stockings. Her legs were now bare, her skin pale and smooth and...

"Any theory on who the buyer was?"

"No. We've been looking at a number of groups, both foreign and domestic. Thesing had recently aligned himself with environmental causes."

"And that was four months ago?" Beth clarified, obviously trying to figure out the connection between what he was telling her and Rabbit Rheaume and even herself. And also possibly recognizing that for months now the terrorism alert level had remained in the elevated level, when, given the situation, it should have been much higher.

Mark straightened. "We've been chasing leads with little progress. Recently, because continued Intel hasn't picked up any mention of the theft or the weapon, we had started to theorize that Thesing may have had second thoughts and either destroyed the MX141 or possibly hidden it somewhere. That his death had been a result of his refusal to turn it over to the buyer."

Leaning forward, he propped his elbows on his knees and met her gaze. "And then just this morning I received a call from Rabbit Rheaume's attorney. Rheaume claimed to have been approached in early July by a man looking to sell MX141. In exchange for the prosecution dropping a number of charges, Rheaume would give us his identity."

Her shoulders dropped slightly. "And now Rabbit is dead?" As if she'd noticed his previous interest in her legs, she tugged at the hem of the navy-blue skirt, tucking one ankle in even more tightly behind the other.

It was a prim-and-proper pose that he suspected she'd

perfected during the years when she'd acted as her father's unofficial hostess following her mother's death.

"And you don't really think it's a coincidence. You think whoever has the chemical weapon knew Rheaume was about to give him up?"

"The timing and the way it went down certainly leaves open the possibility."

Her eyes narrowed. "How did it happen?"

"An inmate using a shiv got Rabbit in the jugular. He was dead before prison guards could get to him."

"And the inmate? Did you question him?"

"Didn't get the chance. A guard shot him." Mark clasped his hands in front of him. "Right now we're interviewing any recent visitors the inmate had, but there's only a few and none of them look promising."

Her eyes narrowed. "If it was a hit, someone would have needed to contact him to set it up, wouldn't they?"

"Sure. But it looks as if there may have been a middle man, another inmate who was involved. A go-between. Who, even if we're lucky enough to ID him, obviously isn't going to talk. At least not right away."

She nodded. "So you're hoping I can help in some way?"

"At the time of the theft and the possible contact between our unsub and Rheaume, you would have still been working the money laundering case. Any chance you saw or heard anything?"

Beth's mouth tightened briefly before she answered. "I saw and heard a lot during those eighteen months as Rabbit's assistant, but unfortunately, none of it pointed to Rabbit's involvement in the sale of any type of weapon, even assault rifles. And certainly nothing like a chemical weapon."

Obviously it wasn't what he wanted to hear. "You're certain?"

"Absolutely certain?" She hedged. "No. Of course not. Even though I was involved in most aspects of his business, I imagine there were instances where that wasn't the case. Rabbit was the cautious sort. He built himself a pretty good niche business laundering money for half a dozen mid-level drug traffickers. He wouldn't do business with large ones because they were the ones the feds were after. And he refused to take on a partner. Which is why he managed to fly under the radar for so many years and why it was so difficult to get the evidence needed to prosecute him. All that being said, though, I just can't see his having the type of contacts who would deal in chemical weapons."

She leaned back. "My guess, for what it's worth, is Rabbit somehow heard about the theft and decided to use it to his advantage."

This time when her mouth tightened, his gaze lingered on her lips for several seconds before he caught himself and forced his eyes to meet hers again. "A deal would have been contingent on the info panning out."

"Even if it didn't, he would have had some fun messing with the feds. Rabbit likes—" She broke off to correct herself. "Rabbit liked to mess with people. He really enjoyed watching them squirm. He was cruel like that."

She glanced away, her voice dropping. "One minute he'd be chatting you up, the next he'd have your face in the dirt and a gun muzzle planted against the back of your skull."

Because he'd read her file, he knew she was speaking from personal experience.

Getting to her feet, she motioned toward the kitchen. "The coffee should be ready by now. If you're in a hurry," she said over her shoulder, "I can put it in a to-go cup."

She wanted him gone. Unfortunately, there was at least one more thing he needed to discuss with her. "No. I'm not in any hurry."

After pouring two cups, she handed one to him, then retreated with the other to lean against the opposite counter. The harsh fluorescent lighting revealed the shadows beneath her eyes. She'd had a rough night, maybe a couple of rough years. Eighteen months undercover, constantly on edge, continually fearful of taking a wrong step, would have been a difficult assignment for even a seasoned agent, let alone one with just over a year's worth of experience.

Why had she been chosen for the assignment?

He set his cup on the counter. "I think there may be one possibility you haven't yet considered."

"What's that?" She blew on her coffee.

"If Rabbit Rheaume wasn't lying, if he was killed to keep him from talking… Maybe it wasn't Rabbit behind what happened to you tonight."

Something flashed briefly in her eyes. Renewed fear maybe, but then it was gone. She took a quick sip and then lowered the cup. "So you're theorizing that whoever silenced Rabbit is now trying to do the same to me? Because he believes I know something?"

"I think you have to consider the possibility. Especially given that Rabbit contacted us today and not a week from now. Why, after arranging your death, not wait to hear if Leon Tyber was successful? If he had been, there'd have been no need to contact us. To get messed up in any of this.

At least, that's my understanding. That without your testimony there was a good chance the prosecution wouldn't get a conviction."

She seemed to contemplate what he'd said for several seconds, and then just as quickly discarded it. "Thanks for the warning, but I'm putting my money on Rabbit. And even if I'm wrong, whoever your unsub is, he's not stupid. He's got to realize that if I did have any information, I would have already shared it. If not before tonight, certainly during this visit."

Looking down at her coffee, she pushed away from the cabinetry before lifting her chin, meeting his eyes. "Besides, nothing has really changed. I've been looking over my shoulder for months now. I'll just keep doing it."

Her calm composure didn't particularly surprise him. In essence, she was right. Nothing had really changed for her. "It still might be a good idea to stay with a friend for the next few days. Or maybe even your father. If you want, I could talk to Bill Monroe about a few days—"

She cut him off, her voice sharp. "I'll be fine." Her mouth briefly tightened as if she regretted her tone. "Now, if you don't mind, I'd like to get some sleep."

"That's not a bad idea. For both of us. I have an early flight tomorrow, and I'm sure after everything that's happened, you must be beat."

She remained silent. He'd been about to suggest he could sleep on her couch, an offer that, given everything he'd seen and heard to date, she wasn't likely to appreciate.

He dumped what remained of his coffee into the stainless steel sink. But when he turned back to her, something in her expression stopped him from heading for the door. "What is it?"

Beth's eyes narrowed. "Did Rabbit say he'd actually met with the seller?"

"Why?"

"There was one call." She started to bring the mug up to her lips again, but then suddenly lowered it. "It came in on July fifth. The man wouldn't give his name, insisted on talking only to Rabbit."

Mark noticed that her voice shook slightly now and that the knuckles on the hand grasping the mug were pale. As if it wasn't just the cup she was trying to hold on to, but her composure, too. It was a definite departure from her behavior of several seconds ago. As much as he would have liked to be concerned about the emotional shift, he couldn't be right now.

"Did he take the call?"

She nodded. "In his private office. Afterward, when he came out, he was in a mood and said something about having limits." She put the mug down and crossed her arms in front of her. "And that some things weren't for sale."

The fifth… The theft had occurred on the second, so the timing made it possible. And since she'd provided a date, going through the calls from that day wouldn't take much effort. But why would she find a discussion about a phone call from four months ago unsettling? Maybe when he heard it, he'd have a better understanding.

"I'll need you to listen to the recordings from that day. Tell me which—"

"There aren't any."

"What do you mean? Certainly if there was an ongoing investigation—"

"There was a problem with the phone taps. I'd just been alerted to the situation and assumed the call, the one we're talking about, was somehow connected to the problem. That my cover had been blown." She grimaced. "Which turned out to be true, but not until much later."

"But you're fairly confident now that the call wasn't related to your cover, but to something else?"

"I'm not certain, no. But looking back, recalling Rabbit's behavior, I don't think he knew until that afternoon that I was a fed. He wasn't usually the patient sort."

"You mean because he didn't confront you until later."

She offered up a wry smile. "Yeah. Because the *incident* didn't take place until later." Her emphasis on the word seemed to suggest something, but he didn't allow himself to get sidetracked.

"I assume the phone company had a trap on the line, too?"

She offered a stiff nod. "Sure. And we got a phone number. Unfortunately, it belonged to a public pay phone outside a laundromat."

He inhaled sharply. Jesus. He couldn't recall the last time he'd worked a case like this one, where he was thwarted at every turn. "I know I'm talking a long shot here, but is there any possibility that you could recognize the voice if you heard it again?"

For several seconds she continued to meet his gaze and then, tightening her arms in front of her, she closed her eyes. Her brows drew down over them, her head cocking ever so slightly to the left. As if she listened to something only she could hear.

Waiting for her response, his gaze dipped to her mouth. Her lips were softly full, the remnants of lipstick clinging to the shapely outer edges. As he watched, they parted, the tip of her tongue running along the lower one briefly before disappearing again.

His pulse had immediately accelerated as he watched, but it was several seconds before he realized that more than just his heart had been impacted. Fighting the tension in his lower body, he averted his eyes.

He found himself recalling the last time he'd reacted similarly to a woman. It had been nineteen months, three days and counting.

And because he'd allowed himself to get distracted, she was dead. It was that final memory that destroyed whatever sexual tension remained, leaving behind the cold emptiness he'd come to accept as a necessity. Because it allowed him to do his job.

When he lifted his chin, his eyes met her slightly narrowed ones. He got the oddest sensation that she somehow knew where his thoughts had gone.

She inhaled sharply, looking slightly unsettled. "Would I recognize the voice? Maybe."

LESS THAN SEVEN hours later at 4:30 a.m. Mark was in the hotel exercise room, wrapping up mile four on the treadmill while Colton Larson sat on the edge of a bench working with free weights. Because of the early hour, they had the relatively soundproof space to themselves.

A television mounted high in one corner was tuned to CNN, but the volume was turned off, the closed caption scrambling across the bottom of the screen. Mark read the story covering a congressional investigation. "Another lobbyist bites the dust."

Larson was still too focused on what they'd been talking about before, though, to show any interest in the Carson scandal.

"I can't believe you're even considering this," Larson

said. "Adding Beth Benedict to the team." The dumbbell he'd been using made a soft *thump* and *clang* as he exchanged it for a heavier one. "I'm not downplaying her language skills. Or suggesting that they aren't ones that we're in need of since Ledbetter was pulled off the team. But her background is in forensic accounting, for godsake, not counterterrorism."

"She was at the top of her class three years ago. She impressed not just me but her other instructors, too."

Larson's mouth tightened. "I'm just questioning if she's the best we can do. If one of us has to break pace to bring her up to date on four months of investigation, you're not really adding manpower, you're losing it. At least temporarily."

Mark upped the treadmill speed, lengthening his stride into a full sprint. He understood Larson's reservations because he shared a number of them. "I haven't made any kind of decision yet."

With an intense expression, Larson pumped away. Sweat collected at the end of his nose. He blew out, dislodging it. "Bill Monroe isn't an idiot. If he's limiting her to administrative duties and has her seeing a shrink, there's a reason." Larson released the twenty-pound weight and straightened. "And from what I hear, she was so spooked by getting locked in that car trunk, she can't even get on a damn elevator. You're going to have a hard time finding anyone who wants her covering their back."

Everything Larson said was true. She wasn't an ideal choice. In fact, when Mark had been working his way down the pro and con list at 3:00 a.m., the cons had been a runaway train. Her emotional health was questionable; she didn't have a background in counterterrorism; not one of his agents would be eager to work with her.

And as far as recognizing the voice on the phone that day, even if she had the ability, it wouldn't do them any good until they had a suspect in custody, and even then it was unlikely to be admissible in court. On top of all those things there was nothing to say with any certainty that the call was even related to the current situation.

In the pro column, though, she would bring something to the table that no other candidate could.

Mark adjusted the treadmill speed downward, slowing his pace. "I think you're overlooking one crucial fact. She may be the only connection we have to our unsub. If it wasn't Rabbit who hired Leon Tyber, but our unsub, there's always the possibility he'll come after her again."

"I agree. Use her as bait. But that doesn't necessarily require that she be part of the team. If the unsub wants her dead, he's just as likely to go after her here in Baltimore. Ask that she be placed under constant surveillance."

Larson was right. Mark could handle it that way, but he wouldn't. He grabbed a towel from the basket next to the door and wiped down. He'd request that Beth be added to the team this morning before leaving Baltimore.

As it had several times since he'd left her place last night, his mind drifted slightly off-topic and into more personal avenues, where he wasn't so much thinking about her as an agent but as a woman. Even during their short conversation, he'd found himself distracted more than once by her attractiveness. It seemed reasonable to assume her presence would impact at least a few members of his team in the same way.

He had just draped the towel around his neck when his cell phone went off. Even as he reached for it, he and Larson glanced toward the television, focusing on the closed caption, looking for the kind of bad news that would lead to a predawn call, but the text at the bottom of the screen still dealt with the lobbying scandal.

The ringer sounding a third time, Mark checked the number to the incoming call. It was his SAC, special agent in charge, David Daughtry.

As he listened to what Daughtry had to say, the knot in Mark's chest—the one he'd been battling recently—tightened. He sank onto the closest bench. Larson sat only a few feet away having abandoned his weights, his elbows propped on his knees as he listened.

Even from the one-sided conversation, it would be obvious to him that after months of chasing a ghost, they'd officially run out of time. The investigation had suddenly rocketed into a whole new phase. With even higher stakes.

Disconnecting less than three minutes later, Mark dragged the towel from around his neck and tossed it toward the hamper. Bellingham, North Carolina. He'd never heard of it, had no idea what larger, more-familiar city it was located near. He soon would.

When was the last time he visited a city, a town, a destination where something bad hadn't just happened? When was the last time he'd climbed onto a plane with a bathing suit and not a business suit packed in his luggage?

Larson's face had gone from flushed to pale. "It's finally happened, hasn't it?"

"Too early to be certain. Call came in just over an hour ago, requesting our assistance."

"Where?"

"Bellingham, North Carolina." Mark tried to breathe past the knot. "A high school."

Larson swiped the sweat from his face with a single hand. "How many casualties?"

Mark climbed to his feet. "Two."

Still sitting, Larson looked up in surprise, his eyes narrowing in disbelief. "Only two?"

Two casualties. Mark knew he should be relieved by the number, but somehow it didn't make any difference. Even two was too many.

Taking a deep breath, he then let it out slowly. The maneuver didn't help. The tightness in his chest was still there. "Obviously, if it was MX141, it's just a warm-up exercise."

Chapter Four

Breathing hard, Beth hefted the sledgehammer to waist level, her right hand choking down near the steel head, her left one sliding to the very end of the wooden shaft before tightening. A radio tuned to a rock station blared in the background, and construction dust floated around her. Good thing her neighbors were out of town.

The decision to take out the wall between her kitchen and the small breakfast room had been a spur-of-the-moment one when she couldn't sleep. Perhaps it was a bigger project than was sensible to take on like that, but she'd needed some kind of physical activity to block out the nonproductive thoughts that had been plaguing her since Mark's departure.

When she'd last checked it had been 4:00 a.m., but that probably had been more than an hour ago. In another thirty minutes or so, she'd need to shower and get dressed. Start psyching herself up for another round of questioning by some of Baltimore PD's finest and for a face-to-face with Bill Monroe. The first wouldn't require much in the way of preparation, but the latter would. Undoubtedly, Monroe would find some way to turn last night's attempt on her life to his advantage.

She nudged aside the two-by-four that had fallen, widening her stance once more as she studied the framing above the doorway. She'd been at the demolition for possibly three hours now and her muscles were beginning to slow even if her mind wasn't.

"Name three things—" she heaved in a breath "—that are deader than a doornail."

She'd lost track of the times she'd ticked off the first two. Leon Tyber. Rabbit Rheaume. And since it was only her testimony during Rheaume's upcoming trial that had been keeping Bill Monroe in check, her career was likely to be number three on the hit list.

Unless Mark intervened.

But that still didn't justify what she'd done. She'd intentionally misled him when she'd said she might be able to recognize the voice if she heard it again—an exaggeration born of a desperate desire to save her career. A prime example of careerism.

Her gut roiled with guilt. She'd sat there in the garage tonight with Tom, acting as if she possessed more integrity, pretending that her principles were superior to his, when in reality they weren't.

Her biceps and shoulder muscles tensed as she lifted the sledgehammer higher still, taking careful aim. She put all her weight and upper-body strength into the swing, but as soon as iron struck wood, she quickly stepped back. The loosened chunk of framing slammed to the floor, kicking up a small cloud of plaster dust.

What if Mark had known he was being manipulated? And even if he hadn't, even if he bought the idea that she might recognize the voice, would he be likely to go to Bill Monroe?

If not, her awkward attempt to save her job wasn't going to be worth squat. It would be only a matter of time before she was sent for a fitness-for-duty exam. She wouldn't be surprised to learn that Bill Monroe was already making the arrangements. Which meant that in a matter of weeks, even before Christmas rolled around, she could be out of a job.

The idea left her feeling as if she'd been sliced open, twenty feet of gut pulled out and run through a meat grinder. From the time she'd been eleven and had written to the FBI, asking for a silhouette target, she had dreamed of becoming an agent. She had worked hard, acquiring skills to give herself the all-important leg up over the competition.

And now it was very likely going to be taken away from her. Just like that. Because she'd confronted Bill Monroe. Because she'd believed the oath she'd taken to protect the American public was a sacred one—more important than anything else…even the survival of her career.

Recognizing that she'd allowed her thoughts once more to get bogged down in things she had no control over, she shifted her grip on the sledgehammer.

Maybe what she needed to worry about was how she was going to live with herself if Mark did believe her. She'd lied to a man whom she held in great respect. She was intentionally trying to use him to save her ass. Both of which made her extremely uncomfortable.

She heaved out a breath. "Let's not pull punches here. Everything about the man makes you uncomfortable." That damn intense gaze. Those probing questions. And that lean body was pretty damn hard to ignore, too. All those lovely muscles…

She suddenly realized she was about to start down yet

another wrong road, one with even less value than the previous one. What she needed to do was remain completely focused on the really important things right now.

"Name four things that are deader than a doornail…Leon. Rabbit. Your career." Ducking her head, she used her forearm to wipe sweat from her forehead. "And coming in at number four on tonight's big countdown…what's left of your integrity."

Negotiating around the debris, she raised the sledgehammer into position again, her shoulder muscles fighting to retain control.

"Name five things that are deader than a doornail…"

Here was where it got scarier. At least on a personal level. If Mark was right, if it hadn't been Rabbit behind the attempt on her life tonight, there was every possibility that she'd be number five on her own list.

When Mark had first posed the potential risk, it hadn't really unsettled her. Because it had seemed as if nothing had really changed. For four months now she'd been looking over her shoulder, believing Rheaume might try to have her killed. But now that she'd given it some more consideration, she realized that it was different. Seriously different.

As crazy as it was on a subconscious level at least, she hadn't been overly afraid of Rabbit. Because she'd survived his first attempt to kill her, she felt more confident that she would be victorious again if put to the test.

But they were no longer talking a midlevel money launderer out to get her. They were talking terrorists here. The real deal.

Definitely not a comfortable thought.

Dropping the sledgehammer, she left it standing on its

head as she stepped around the fifty-five-gallon trash can to reach the bottle of water on the counter. She tugged off the face mask, leaving it dangling around her neck.

It was as she took the first swig that the room's condition registered fully. Believing her safety glasses responsible for most of the fuzziness, she removed them. The haziness remained. And that was only the beginning. Dark electrical wires dangled from the ceiling like long tentacles, their safely capped ends of neon yellow and orange swaying slightly. Pebblelike chunks of plaster had fallen out of the lath as she'd ripped the ceiling down and now resembled gravel strewn across the old floor.

Reaching over, she turned down the radio. What in the hell had she been thinking? Starting a demolition when there was a chance that she'd have to put her house on the market? No job, therefore no money for mortgage.

But as with most things in her life right now, there obviously was no turning back.

As she reached for the sledge again, someone pounded on the front door. She glanced at the clock—5:55 a.m. Who the hell…?

Dread beginning to pool at her core, she shed the safety glasses and retrieved the .45 automatic—her home-protection weapon—from the counter.

Maybe it was just a neighbor in trouble, but she didn't think so. Given the past twelve hours, she felt fairly certain Mark had been right. That Rabbit had nothing to do with the attempt on her life. That someone had come to correct Leon Tyber's mistake.

Flicking off the safety, she pulled aside the plastic sheeting she'd used to seal the kitchen from the rest of the house and stepped into the hall. There were no lights on in this part of the house, and she left it that way, preferring not to give whoever was out there a heads-up.

She took up a precautionary position just to the right of the door and out of the direct line of fire in case the person on the other side was planning to pump a few rounds through the solid wood panel. Whoever it was had finally located the door buzzer and punched it a dozen times in rapid succession. Her already fatigued muscles contracted as if the zaps of sound were short blasts of electric current.

Taking a deep breath, she shifted her index finger from the trigger guard to the trigger. "Who is it?" she called through the door.

"Mark Gerritsen."

The sound of his voice only served to make the adrenaline kick a little faster. What would he be doing here at this time of morning? She hadn't anticipated any additional contact with him, at least not right away. As she'd shown him out last night, he'd mentioned having to catch an early flight to Boston.

"Beth?"

"Give me a sec." Still holding the automatic, she punched in the security code to the alarm system and then worked the dead bolt.

As soon as she had the door open, almost before she had time to move aside, he slipped past her, accompanied by a gust of frigid air.

He was dressed in a suit and an overcoat. If not for the fact that he was clean shaven and that he smelled of soap, shampoo and cologne, she might have questioned if he'd been to bed since she'd last seen him.

In sharp contrast to his impeccable grooming, she wore

paint-spattered, low-rise sweatpants, an old FBI T-shirt that she'd long ago cropped and a face mask clogged with construction dust. And since she hadn't bothered to brush her hair when she climbed out of bed it was matted to her skull. Not exactly how any woman wanted to be caught. Especially by an attractive, well-dressed male.

"You should try answering your phone," he offered tersely, his brows drawn down tight over his eyes.

What in the world was with him? Just because she hadn't answered her phone at an unreasonable hour, he decided to drive all the way out here at this time of morning? And then is irritated…? She frowned. Was it possible that when he hadn't been able to reach her, he'd grown concerned? She found the possibility that he might have been checking on her intriguing.

By the time she turned around again, he'd wandered as far as the kitchen doorway and was pulling aside the plastic sheeting. Before she could stop him, he ducked through.

Obviously, he expected her to follow. For a brief moment she debated staying where she was, forcing him to return to the foyer, but then decided playing power games with Mark as an adversary was stupid at best. Mostly because she was unlikely to win, and it would eat up time better spent getting ready for work.

She jerked off the face mask and then, tugging up the neck of her T-shirt almost as if she was stripping it off, she used the less dusty inside to wipe her face before following him into the kitchen. "What's going on?"

"I could ask the same thing." He glanced at her. "Is this your idea of midnight therapy?"

Midnight therapy? For the second time in a matter of minutes, she scanned the mess she'd created, recognizing how it must appear to an outsider. To Mark. As if she'd lost her mind. And maybe she had.

Screw it. He was going to think what he was going to think.

Stepping past him, she turned off the radio. "I hadn't planned to start demolition until this weekend." The lie came with surprising ease. "But physical activity helps me think."

She folded her arms across her, her forearms settling against her bare midriff. "Now what's going on?" she repeated. "I know you're not here to discuss my renovation schedule."

She saw indecision in his eyes, as if he was wondering the same thing—why in the hell he was there. Or maybe he actually had been concerned about her, but for obvious reasons was now hesitant to admit it.

"You've been assigned to the task force, and there's been a development. You need to get packed."

"I've been what?" She managed to keep her voice in check, but certainly not her thoughts.

She hadn't given any consideration to the possibility he might actually request her transfer. The most she'd anticipated was a reprieve. One that would give her some time and a shot at another investigation where she could shine in her field—in forensic accounting. Which wasn't likely to happen in a counterterrorism outfit where the other team members would have been handpicked because of their extensive knowledge of terrorist groups and activities.

"I requested your reassignment," he clarified.

In the middle of the night? Had he awakened Bill Monroe? Or someone at FBI headquarters? Normally a transfer didn't happen instantaneously, and the idea that this one had left her feeling uncertain.

Her eyes narrowed. "Why would you do that?" It didn't

surprise her that he had pull, but that he would use it to get her transferred did. What could be that urgent? Then she replayed everything in her head a second time. "You said there's been a development. What kind?"

His eyes met hers, but there was a disconnect in them that hadn't been there earlier tonight. A sense that he saw her, but that he was no longer emotionally involved with her on a human level.

So it hadn't been concern for her after all. She was caught off guard by the level of her disappointment.

"I'll fill you in on the plane. Right now you need to get cleaned up and packed."

Tightening her arms, she lifted her chin. "I think you need to know that I may have misled you somewhat about my ability to recognize the voice."

"That has nothing to do with the reason I made the request."

"Then what does?"

"Whoever wants you dead… If they sent someone after you once, they may do it again. If they do, we've got a shot at getting to them before…" Mark didn't finish the thought.

Why not finish it? What exactly had happened? And then the last pieces fell into place.

"It's happened, hasn't it?"

"Maybe. We're waiting for the FBI lab to make the confirmation. Now get dressed."

Beth shoved the gun into her waistband. At least now she knew why he hadn't finished his earlier statement. And the reason for the disconnect in his eyes. She had suddenly become a means to an end. An instrument he could use. That he could exploit.

She jerked off the mask, dropped it on the pile of rubble. "So you want to use me as bait?"

His mouth tightened. "Sweetheart, you *are* bait. I can't change that. But I fully intend to take advantage of it."

Chapter Five

Ducking because of the limited headroom, Mark walked up the tight aisle of the Cessna Citation. The pilot, a man in his early thirties, glanced up from the instrument panel. Seeing Mark, he flipped the mike away from his lips.

"We'll be taking off in the next ten to fifteen minutes. We've got some more weather coming in from the west, so the ride's going to be bumpy. You might want to grab coffee and a doughnut from the beverage center before we get in the air." He motioned to the magazine rack. "I shoved a *USA TODAY* in there somewhere, too. Help yourself."

"Thanks." After digging out the newspaper, Mark bypassed the first seat because it faced backward. He preferred to see where he was going.

Larson had followed him onboard. Still talking on a cell phone, he dropped down into the seat facing Mark's, leaving Beth five more to choose from.

She hesitated just inside the door, one hand resting on a seat back as she gave quick consideration to her options. Mark saw her gaze briefly connect with Larson as she took the seat across the aisle from Mark's.

When she and Larson had met fifteen minutes ago, he

hadn't bothered to hide his opinion of her. Or of Mark's decision to add her to the unit. She'd handled the rebuff surprisingly well, and had maintained a professional aloofness since.

It was the third time in twelve hours that she'd remained cool in the face of significant pressure. It wasn't enough to allay all his concerns about her mental fitness— he still intended to monitor her every move—but it did make him wonder if Bill Monroe might be after her for more personal reasons.

There was a slight bang and thump as the outside door was sealed and then the usual fuselage shimmy as turbo-props were revved. Because of the frigid outside tempera-tures, the interior was cool and would probably remain that way through much of the flight.

After buckling up, she retrieved the case notes he'd given her earlier from her briefcase. It wasn't a particularly detailed breakdown of the investigation, but it did provide the basics on the dead chemist Harvey Thesing's back-ground and a brief recap of his known associates, includ-ing business ones past and present, friends, family and fellow tree huggers.

All of them had been interviewed at least once and several of them had received repeated visits from the task force.

Along with those notes were the ones on MX141. She'd still be at a disadvantage, but it was the best he could do. As Larson had noted, Mark couldn't afford to waste manpower bringing her completely up to speed.

Besides, ask anyone in law enforcement—being a good investigator was as much about gut instinct and reading people as it was about anything else. From what he'd seen to date, she was well equipped in both departments.

As Larson ended his call, turning off the phone before clipping it to his belt again, Mark motioned toward the re-freshment center. "There's coffee and doughnuts."

Larson grimaced. It was the reaction Mark had expected from the other man.

A year ago Larson wouldn't have passed up a doughnut or two or three. That had changed after his divorce. He'd suddenly gone healthy. Not just with his eating habits but with a strict exercise regimen, too. Which wasn't easy to maintain in the midst of a major investigation.

Mark turned to Beth. "What about you? I didn't give you much of a chance to get breakfast."

She shook her head and offered a vague smile, followed by a polite "No, thanks."

Settling back, she opened up the report. She was trying to appear at ease, but she wasn't. And if he had to make a guess, he'd have said it was the plane making her that way. Had small planes always bothered her, or was it something to do with the more-recent issue of claustrophobia?

Larson rubbed his hands together. "A bit chilly in here, isn't it?" He glanced over at Beth with a too-eager smile. "You okay?"

She looked up with a frown. "Sure. Why wouldn't I be?"

"I don't know. Some people have problems with small planes. With tight, confining spaces and nothing but empty air under their asses. It's sort of like an elevator," he said, smiling, "only there're a lot more floors between you and the basement."

She offered up a bland expression. "Interesting analogy." Without waiting for a response, she went back to the report.

Despite the continued tension between them, Mark

didn't plan to interfere. He suspected Beth wouldn't appreciate it if he did. And she might as well get used to it. Most of the unit wouldn't see her as a welcome addition. If she wanted their respect, she was going to have to earn it the same way the rest of them had. With her performance.

Crosswinds made taking off tricky, but once in the air the ride smoothed out some.

"What's the status?" Mark asked. He wanted to find out what Larson had just learned, but because the pilot might overhear them, he needed to keep the conversation as oblique as possible. "Has HMRU reached the scene yet?"

Even if the FBI lab's toxicology report had yet to be completed, the Hazardous Material Response Unit would be able to do a field verification. It wouldn't be extremely accurate, but at least they'd know if it was a nerve agent that they were dealing with and not some other compound.

"They're set to arrive in Bellingham before us. If we're lucky, we'll know something by the time we're on the ground, but no promises. And if we're really lucky, the medical examiner got it all wrong."

Mark nodded. As much as he would have liked the medical examiner to have made a mistake, Mark doubted that was the case. Even medical examiners in rural areas would recognize the differences between pesticide poisoning and one caused by a nerve agent.

Mark shifted the conversation. "Any news on Becky's application?" Larson's sister was nearly nine months into the FBI's rigorous application process.

"She just heard yesterday. Starts training next month. She wanted me to thank you for writing that recommendation."

"Sure."

"Know anything about Bellingham?" Larson asked.

"I know the local airstrip is on the short size and can handle only turboprops."

Normally Mark would have obtained at least a minimal amount of information on their destination. It tended to help in determining the best approach for establishing rapport with local law enforcement.

Large urban departments tended to be better organized and their personnel to be more highly trained. He found that with them he didn't have to watch what he said. They were up-to-date on current techniques and common law enforcement acronyms and oftentimes provided excellent reports and Intel.

On the other hand, with rural departments he tended to stick to more layman-type terms. The last thing he wanted to do as an outsider was to make a local officer feel dumb and get less cooperation.

Without looking up from the MX141 report, Beth said, "Bellingham's population at the last census was eight thousand. They're mostly an agricultural community, with some light industry. Bellingham Police Department's current roster includes seven deputies who respond to calls within the city limits. Unincorporated areas are patrolled by the county sheriff's department. Statistically they're a low-crime area although they had one murder last year. The police chief is Ramsey Livengood. Given the time constraints, I wasn't able to locate anything on his credentials."

Though pleased that she'd done so well, Mark was careful to keep the smile off his face. "Anything else?"

Beth still didn't look up. "The local high school basketball team, the Bellingham Bullets, won the state championship last year and hall-of-famer center Scotty Tiles is from Bellingham."

She flipped the page on the MX141 report. "As far as accommodation there's one chain hotel located in town. It even has an on-site health spa." She glanced up, hitting Larson with a neutral expression. "Should I schedule a seaweed wrap for you?"

Larson's gaze flicked between Mark and Beth, before settling on her face. His brows dropped over his deep-set eyes and he served up a stiff smile. "Thanks. But I can make my own appointments."

"Suit yourself."

Obviously her intention had been to return the favor— to get under Larson's skin some—but she'd been smart enough not to use anything connected to the investigation. Instead she'd utilized something that Larson wouldn't willingly repeat to the rest of the team.

Even after she returned her attention to the MX141 report, Mark continued to study her. She had an almost straight nose and a determined chin with the faintest of clefts. It was a strong profile for a woman. And at the same time, her dark hair somehow managed to soften the effect, as did her lips. It was a face that Mark found arresting. And not just because the bits and pieces made a pretty picture, but because of the intelligence and the resolve he saw in her gray eyes.

She'd cost him quite a bit of sleep last night, trying to decide what to do about her. The phone call this morning had effectively resolved the issue, though. Up until then he'd been trying to factor her best interests into the equation. But with the possible tragedy in Bellingham, he could no longer afford to. It was the country's interests, its safety, that came first. Personal sacrifice was expected. She'd taken the same oath that he had.

So why did using her as bait make him so damned uneasy? Especially when she seemed onboard with it?

Out of his peripheral vision, he caught Larson watching him speculatively. As if he recognized Mark's interest was more personal than it should be. Closing his eyes, Mark rested his head against the seat back, intent on getting a couple of hours rest.

But no matter how hard he tried to concentrate on the faint drone of the engines, he was unsuccessful. As soon as his eyes had shut, another sense kicked into hyperdrive, the scent of her perfume reaching him. At first it was a seemingly subtle one—clean, slightly floral. But then as he sat there, he picked up an underlying layer, one that wasn't quite so innocent. Slightly musky. Sensual.

He found himself wondering where she placed it. Behind the ears? Did she use a finger to dab it there before dragging it slowly forward along her jawline, canting her head slightly, exposing the pale skin of her neck…an offering…

He swallowed roughly.

Or did she put it in the hollow at the base of her throat, trailing it downward across velvety skin… He recalled how she'd been dressed this morning—the toned, bare midriff bisected by a line of perspiration. Suddenly he was envisioning the perfume trail dipping even lower… His chest tightened and his respiration quickened.

Straightening in his seat, he glanced out the window.

What in the hell was wrong with him?

BELLINGHAM HIGH SCHOOL was a large brick structure, the architecture reminiscent of Ivy League colleges. The school stood four miles outside of town and on a slight bluff overlooking fertile lowlands. At this time of year only the remnants of recently harvested crops remained, waiting for spring when they would be tilled back into the black soil, adding nitrogen.

Larson and Beth had already reached the front door when Mark turned and hesitated on the wide granite steps, the duffle containing his hazmat gear almost forgotten in his hand as he studied the picturesque town in the distance. Two church spires, nearly side by side, rose up through the scrabble of bare-limbed trees and into the cloudless sky. It was the type of scene that almost made it possible to believe everything was right in the world. But it wasn't.

Since that hot July night when he'd first learned of MX141, Mark had been waiting for the call. He just never expected it to bring him to someplace like Bellingham.

To make matters worse, some higher-up, citing concerns of a public panic, had ordered the Hazardous Material Response Unit to stand down until either the FBI lab or Mark verified a credible threat.

A mixture of frustration and anger pumped through him. Only minutes ago he'd received the detailed toxicology report on his PDA. There was no longer any doubt. Whoever had acquired MX141, they'd chosen Bellingham as their first target.

The federal Hazmat Response Unit and the task force were now en route, but critical time had been wasted.

Shifting his gaze, he stared at the county road where media vans were beginning to stack up. A television cameraman had now climbed onto the roof of his vehicle, his camera briefly aimed at the front of the school. At Mark.

In a matter of hours he would have to do the impossible—compose a statement that wasn't going to send the whole nation into a panic. And at the moment he still had no idea if they were dealing with home-grown terrorists or foreign ones.

Statistically, terrorist activity within U.S. borders was more likely to be carried out by extremists. By antigovernment groups. Animal-rights activists. Abortion opponents. And hard-line environmentalists. Since, in the months prior to the theft and Thesing's murder, the chemist had aligned himself with the latter, Mark kept coming back to that possibility. Because it made the most sense.

"Gerritsen?" Larson prompted.

Turning away from the view, Mark jogged up the remaining stairs. "No guard."

He'd expected to find the site sealed up, but so far the only form of security they'd encountered was the barricades across the entrance road. They'd easily driven around them. It wouldn't be long before the media did the same.

As Beth reached for the door, Mark took her by the elbow, urging her back to the edge of the landing.

"Why only two victims?" Mark asked as he released her. "Why here?"

She didn't appear to catch on to the reason he'd dragged her out of the shadows next to the building and into the sunshine where she could be seen, could be filmed by the cameraman below.

If the attack last night had been ordered by whoever had the MX141, the more exposure she had, the more likely they were to come after her again.

"Why would a terrorist choose Bellingham?" he prompted.

"Because…" Her eyes narrowed, traveling the same path his had moments earlier, taking in the setting, the crisp, beautiful day. The sound of crows cawing as they settled over the closest field like black snow. "Because no one would anticipate it happening here. Because the terrorists would know that even if the federal government hasn't announced anything to the American people, Homeland Security and the FBI are functioning at high alert, watching the high-profile targets like the New York Stock Exchange, the New York subway system, the White House…" She paused. "And because it buys them time."

A slight breeze lifted her dark hair, a section catching on her lips, forcing her to reach up in an unsuccessful attempt to capture the strands before the wind could again. Last night her hair had appeared to be nearly black, but in the sunlight it came alive with streaks of auburn and gold. And as with most things about her, he noticed more than he should.

"What do you mean?" He fought the urge to offer assistance as she tried to restrain her hair.

She shifted her duffle bag to the opposite hand. "If this had been a large metropolitan city, local law enforcement would have been all over it. It wouldn't have taken days for us to be brought into the investigation, it would have been only hours. Because big-city PDs train for this kind of thing. Places like Bellingham don't."

She impressed him with both the analysis and the way she handled herself. "And the additional time is important because it buys them a window of opportunity, the ability to deliver a second strike almost before we're aware of the first," he added.

"So you're suggesting we should be expecting another one almost immediately?" Larson asked from just behind them.

Mark's mouth thinned. "Yeah. My guess is that we're on borrowed time here. And I think the scope of the next incident and the target will depend on if they view what happened here as a success. Or if they feel their delivery system, or some other aspect needs refinement."

He could think of one more reason that Bellingham might have been chosen, a reason that in many ways was even more sinister. What better method to destroy the last of this country's false sense of security, than to strike middle America? To demonstrate that no one was truly safe. Truly beyond harm's reach?

Larson opened the door and held it for Beth and Mark, before following them into the large, dim space. Glancing up at the fluorescent fixtures more than twelve feet overhead, Mark realized that it wasn't so much a matter of poor lighting as the dark-oak trim and brown floor tiles soaking up the illumination.

The deputy sitting on a folding, metal chair just inside the door lurched to his feet, the heavy leather of his duty belt creaking as if brand-new. It wasn't unusual for police departments in small, rural towns to hire younger officers, and this freckle-faced, rawboned kid looked as if he should still be in high school.

Mark flashed his badge. "I'm Special Agent Mark Gerritsen, and this is Special Agent Colton Larson and Special Agent Beth Benedict. I'd like to see Chief Livengood if he's available."

The young officer lifted his radio to his mouth and made the request. Lowering it, he said, "The chief will be with you in a sec."

Mark nodded. "How much of the building has been sealed off?"

"The gymnasium and the locker rooms."

"But nothing else?" He tried to maintain a conversational tone. It wasn't easy given the situation. The whole structure should have been locked down immediately, no one allowed in. Of course, to be fair to the police chief, initially he'd thought he was dealing with an accidental death and not one caused by a nerve agent. And even now the FBI's soft response to the situation was probably leading him to believe the risk was minimal. Especially after thirty-six hours.

"No, sir." The officer looked slightly nervous now, as if he'd picked up on Mark's disapproval. "But it's only the principal and her secretary who's been in, and they go straight to their offices."

"Both of them are in the building right now, though?"

"Yes…um…yes, sir."

When Mark had walked away, beyond Kid Deputy's hearing, Larson followed. "They have no idea what they're dealing with," he offered quietly. "Shouldn't you order them to evacuate?"

"After the handshake. I prefer not to cut the local police chief off at the knees unless I have to. And you're right, he doesn't have any idea what he's dealing with. Because he and everyone else has been kept in the dark."

It wasn't until he heard the edge of anger in his own voice that he fully realized just how much that infuriated him.

Larson nodded. "I suppose the only danger at this point is if there's more of the stuff on school property that hasn't been discovered."

"If any of it remains in the building, it isn't in the administrative offices. It's in areas frequented by students, the kind of victims who will make people take notice."

While Mark had been talking to the officer and then Larson, Beth had wandered to the long display case stretching along one wall. As she studied the trophies, game balls and team photos, Larson studied her with a shuttered expression. Was it possible that, as much as he might not want to, Larson found her attractive? He'd been divorced for more than a year now, which made it likely that he was dating even if Mark hadn't heard Larson mention a specific woman.

But then, Mark couldn't recall the last time he himself had gone on a second date. Usually by the end of the first one most women were clued in on the type of relationship he was offering—one without expectations on either side.

As his ex-wife had so succinctly put it, absence didn't make the heart grow fonder, it just led to apathy. And as far as he was concerned, there was too damn much of that in the world already.

Larson's eyes continued to track Beth's progress as she followed the display case, pausing every few feet.

"She definitely has a good ass."

The comment irritated Mark. "That's not all she has. She's sharp. Her analysis of why a small town had been chosen was a good one."

Frowning, Larson placed his duffle on the floor. "Maybe she's having a good day."

"Or maybe she has what it takes."

"If you think so, then you should let her watch your back. Because no one else will want her watching their's. Not when it really counts."

It was the second time Larson had brought it up, which bothered Mark to a certain extent. He knew Colton Larson well enough to know that when it really counted, Larson would do the right thing. But when Mark saw Beth's shoulders stiffen as if she'd heard the exchange, it kicked his annoyance to the next level.

"We watch each others' backs. All of us. That hasn't changed. You don't like it…"

"Whoa." Larson held his hands out, palms down. "I just meant that right now her record seems to suggest that she's—"

"Let's stay focused on what's important here. On a good day we're all coping with a hell of a lot of pressure, we don't need to be manufacturing it for each other."

Hearing Chief Ramsey Livengood's approach even before the local cop came into view at the end of the hallway, he chose not to pursue the discussion any further. Larson no doubt had finally gotten the point. They were a team, and as a team they worked together. Seamlessly. Anything short of that wasn't good enough.

The police chief strode toward them, a large manila envelope in his left hand. Mark put his age somewhere in the late fifties, and the combination of high, flat cheekbones and the slightly broad base of his nose suggested Cherokee blood.

Livengood stuck out his right hand. "First off, thanks for coming. Second, I'd appreciate it if you kept me in the loop. This is my beat, my town, you know?"

Mark offered a sharp nod. "Sure. This is Special Agent Larson and Special Agent Benedict."

Even before Livengood's fingers closed around Beth's, he was already staring at her. And then, as if remembering himself, he offered a smile. "Sorry, ma'am. I don't mean to be rude, but you remind me of someone."

"Have you made any additional statements to the press?" Mark asked, wanting to get back on point.

"No. Last one was noon yesterday. I hadn't gotten the call from the ME yet, so we were still calling it accidental." Livengood's mouth flattened. "Once we started thinking about the possibility of a homicide, I figured the less said to news types, the better."

"Good call. Is it possible for me to get a copy of the medical examiner's report, as well as the autopsy findings, any photos taken at the time the bodies were discovered, any background information you have on the victims? And any notes on the case that your men have generated?"

With a smug look, Livengood passed the envelope to Mark. "It's all there. If after you look it over, you need anything additional…"

"I'll be sure to ask," Mark finished. "Now then, I guess the next thing we need is to see where the bodies were found."

"Sure. This way."

As Mark turned to walk with Livengood, Larson and Beth fell in behind. Mark passed the envelope to Beth. "I want the autopsy report on top and the crime-scene photos just beneath. Leave everything else in the envelope for now. I'll take a look at them later." He returned his attention to Livengood. "Maybe you can give me a brief rundown."

"T. J. Duke was a local plumber and the second victim was his helper, Tee Woods. Found them Tuesday close to midnight."

"Who was the first officer on the scene?"

"I was." His expression suggested a wallet or driver's license hadn't been necessary to make the ID.

"And you had no problems with shortness of breath or rapid heart rate?" Beth asked.

Glancing over his shoulder, Livengood shook his head. "No. Nothing like that, ma'am."

The lack of symptoms suggested a significant time lapse between the death of the men and the discovery of their bodies—enough time for the MX141 to have evaporated. Given the closed environment, Mark would estimate three to four hours. Which put the exposure some time before nine o'clock.

"Any idea what they were doing in the building at that time of night?" Mark asked.

"Not for certain. T.J. had been contracted to replumb the showers over the Christmas break, so possibly he'd decided to do some preliminary work."

"But no one saw them arrive?" They were walking past darkened classrooms of empty desks.

"Kids were sent home around ten that morning. Heating system had gone down overnight and the building was too cold to keep them here. Repair people didn't have it up and running again until early afternoon." Livengood slowed. "That was one of the reasons we figured a gas leak of some sort, that the heating guys might have cut a supply line or something."

"What changed your mind?"

Livengood grimaced. "When the medical examiner saw T.J. and Tee—I guess it would have been around three or four in the morning by the time she made it here—she thought it might be some kind of insecticide poisoning. Which got us looking at it as a homicide."

Mark didn't find it surprising that the medical examiner's first thought had been pesticide poisoning. Quite a few of them acted on the nervous system. And with Bellingham being a farm community and with the law of commonality—common things occur commonly— thinking Malathion and not a nerve agent would have been the most logical on-scene assessment.

Livengood jabbed a thumb over his shoulder. "You'll find a breakdown in the packet of T.J.'s and Tee's movements."

Mark scanned the timeline Beth passed to him. At 12:00

p.m. the two men had lunch at Rosie's Lunchbox—the meat loaf special and coffee for the older victim, two slices of apple pie and a milkshake for the younger one. Scanning the rest of the report, Mark realized it was pretty much the same.

As he handed the report back to Beth, Mark kept his expression neutral. There was nothing to be gained by telling Livengood the carefully constructed time line was a waste of time. A couple of plumbers hadn't been the intended target. They'd just been unlucky enough to be in the wrong place at the wrong time.

"It would be helpful to have a list of teachers, the office staff, and anyone who does any type of maintenance for the school. And the name of the outfit that did the heating repair."

"Sure."

Crime-scene tape, stretched between a pair of folding chairs, blocked the entrance to a short hallway and a set of double doors. Livengood scraped one chair aside. "Gymnasium and locker rooms are through there. T.J. and Tee were found in the boys'."

"School was canceled for Tuesday," Mark said. "What about other activities?"

"The basketball team was supposed to have a game. It got rescheduled for tonight."

Mark turned to Beth, retrieving the crime-scene photos and the toxicology report from her. He scanned the toxicology results first, focusing in almost immediately on two key details. The older victim's pant leg and the underlying skin had come into direct contact with a significant amount of MX141 while the younger man's clothing showed no such signs, his death most likely a result of fume inhalation alone.

Mark turned his attention to the top photo.

Livengood started to back away. "I'm late for an appointment with the principal and a couple of school board members. But if you need anything…"

Mark looked up with a frown. "Where's the meeting?"

"The principal's office."

"You should hold it elsewhere." Mark said. "And the game too. Otherwise…"

He held up the photo of the two dead men. "You could have several hundred more bodies like these two."

Chapter Six

Beth studied the crime-scene photo on top of the stack. Two men, one in his early twenties and the other older, were sprawled on a ceramic-tile shower floor, vomit covering their faces and upper bodies, their pants darkened with their own urine.

Her fingers trembled as she imagined the terror they had experienced in the last minutes of their lives. The loss of muscle control. Trapped inside unresponsive bodies. Tortured by the knowledge they were dying, but unable to help themselves.

How could anyone create a chemical that killed so viciously, so quickly? And having created it, how could they fail to keep it safely locked away?

It could have been worse, though.

If the heating system hadn't broken down. If school hadn't been canceled. If the basketball playoff game hadn't been rescheduled. How many more casualties would there have been? A hundred? Several hundred?

The possibility left her shaken.

"Benedict," Mark's low voice interrupted her thoughts. She inhaled past the tightness lingering in her chest.

Flipping the photo to the bottom of the stack, she looked up, surprised to find he'd peeled off his coat, and his duffel stood open at his feet. She obviously knew what he was doing. He was stripping to put on his hazmat suit.

His long fingers dragged the necktie knot steadily downward, finally freeing the tail end. And she'd seen plenty of men remove their neckties…

So why was it that she couldn't seem to treat it like all those other times? And then she realized that it was because there was something almost erotic in the way he did it. Suggestive.

Leaving the tie hanging around his neck, he went to work on the buttons of his conservative shirt.

She desperately needed to turn her attention elsewhere, before he realized the type of thoughts filtering through her mind.

"Get suited up, Benedict," Mark said, glancing up this time. "If you need some help with the gear, Larson will give you a hand."

"No." She managed to slide the photos back into the envelope. "I've got it."

Even if she'd needed help, she wouldn't have accepted it. Not from Larson. She removed her weapon and dropped down, unzipping the canvas satchel. Catching some motion in her peripheral vision, she looked over at Larson. Though he was already in his hazmat suit, he'd yet to close the front zipper, the gaping material revealing his bare chest.

Beth silently cursed her stupidity, her shortsightedness. She should have known she might have to change into gear, but beneath her conservative and heavy navy-blue suit jacket, she wore a barely-there silk camisole and nothing else. No T-shirt. Not even a sports bra.

Maybe she could just leave the coat on beneath the hazmat gear. But even as she considered the option, she knew it would be a mistake. That, at the very least, she'd look stupid. Overly modest.

Larson was already out to get her. And even though the rest of the counterterrorism unit had yet to meet her face-to-face, they would have heard the same rumors—that she was seeing a shrink and wasn't a team player. So the only hope she had of getting the all-male unit to accept her was by proving the rumors wrong. By being the epitome of a team player. By not requesting any type of concession—even one as simple as asking Larson and Mark to turn their backs while she climbed into protective gear. By being "one of the guys."

She dragged the hazmat suit out of the satchel. When Mark had told her about the reassignment, she hadn't known how to feel about it. Reading the report on the plane had changed that, though. She'd joined the FBI because she wanted to make a difference, and the counterterrorism unit was her second chance, her only chance to save her career.

And a little bare skin and some personal embarrassment sure as hell weren't going to stop her.

But a simple gas mask might, she realized.

As far as defining moments went, to anyone not coping with claustrophobia, donning a mask wouldn't seem like much, but to her…

She'd rather face Leon's .45 automatic again.

She tried to calm herself with the knowledge that there was only thirty minutes of air in the preloaded breathing apparatus and that with any luck they might get what they were after even faster than that. But just surviving the thirty minutes wasn't going to be good enough. Somehow, she was going to have to make herself an active participant.

Leaving the protective gear still partially folded at her feet, she straightened and immediately started unbuttoning her jacket. The higher she got, the more her fingers wanted to stumble.

Focus, Benedict.

As she undid the last of them, she heard Larson's zipper scrape upward, the sound climbing her spine like screeching metal. The muscles in her shoulders went tense and there was little hope of relaxing them anytime soon.

Lifting her chin slightly, she shrugged out of her jacket as if she undressed with male agents on a regular basis. The hairs on her arms and her nape lifted as cooler air reached the newly exposed skin. She didn't dare look down. The action would only serve to draw attention to the situation. But she did make the mistake of glancing over as Mark was shedding his shirt. Her breathing took an emphatic, unannounced hitch.

Even in a business suit, it had been obvious that he was well built, but stripped to the waist…

He had broad shoulders and well defined biceps, the kind that would make a woman want to run her hands over them, seeking to feel their resilient strength before moving on to hard pecs and tight male nipples…

It was only when her own abs contracted hard that she managed to look away. Even after she had, keeping her actions unhurried and natural was a challenge. And then as she bent forward to retrieve her gear, the top of the camisole gapped open, her breasts swaying slightly. Maybe it was the cool air reaching them, or the sensation of silk shifting across them. Whatever it was, their tips hardened.

She quickly grabbed the gear and stepped into it. The protective suit was intentionally roomy, but getting it up over her hips without doing the usual female waggle was nearly impossible.

Out of the corner of her eye, she saw Larson strap his weapon back on and grab a handful of evidence bags. She didn't see anything to suggest that he'd noticed her predicament.

Of course, it wasn't as if she had the type of figure that made men sit up and take notice. In fact, the last man she'd dated more than two years ago had summed it up pretty well—firm straight-aways with enough curves to make the trip interesting. Not exactly how any woman wanted to be described.

"All we're looking for at this point," Mark said, "is the method of delivery. How the victims were exposed to the chemical." He looked up from what he was doing, his gaze briefly crossing with hers before shifting to Larson. She realized that even if Mark had glanced at her for a split second, he wasn't actually talking to her. And he wasn't actually expecting anything of her. As far as he was concerned, she was just a piece of frilly bait.

The idea that she was being used wasn't exactly one she was fond of, and something else had been weighing on her mind since this morning, since the reassignment. What if Baltimore PD managed to link Rabbit and Leon? What if it was discovered that it had been Rabbit behind the garage shooting? If that happened, she became useless to Mark for all intents and purposes. She had no reason to believe that he wouldn't see her as dead weight on his team.

But would he immediately cut bait, or would he give her the chance to prove herself?

The next time she looked over, Larson was grabbing his gas mask. Turning he seemed to check out Mark's progress.

"Why don't you go on in, Larson?" Mark said simply as he zipped up and reached for neoprene booties to slide over his shoes. "We'll be there in a minute."

"Sure." Larson slipped on the gas mask with practiced ease, making the adjustments to the fit, checking to be sure that the personal breathing apparatus was working correctly. As he reached for the door handle, he looked back, his eyes skimming both of them. "I'll see you in there."

As she was shoving her arms into the sleeves, her gaze connected with Mark's. Even though it lasted only a second or two, there was no denying the awareness she saw, or the strong ripple of the same springing back to life deep inside her as he continued to study her.

Or the knowledge that if even one member of the task force saw it, there would be no hope of ever gaining their acceptance—the one thing she desperately needed if there was going to be any hope of resurrecting her career.

Grabbing her weapon and mask, she started to follow Larson through the double doors. By now he'd be in the shower room and not in the gymnasium. With any luck she might have a few moments alone to deal with the mask before Mark caught up.

"Aren't you forgetting something, Benedict?"

She managed a quick rundown of equipment before turning to face him. "Such as?"

He tossed her what resembled an oversize ballpoint pen.

Catching it, she realized that it was an autoinjector. And that she had forgotten a critical item. Because she wasn't ready to meet his eyes, she rolled the preloaded dose of antidote back and forth between her fingers and thumb for several seconds as if examining the external markings on the side. "Is it atropine?"

"No." He walked toward her. "It's been specifically developed for MX141." Stopping in front of her, he shoved a second autoinjector into the lapel pocket of the suit. "Do you remember your training? Where to inject yourself if it becomes necessary?"

Her breathing had taken another intense hitch as the pen hit the bottom of the pocket over her right breast. Fighting to control it, she lifted her chin. "Upper thigh muscle."

He stepped back half a step. "Use a smooth thrust and be sure to leave it in place long enough for the antidote to be delivered. From here on out, keep both injectors on you at all times. And if not on you, then within easy reach."

She wanted to be able to tell him that she hadn't suddenly gone stupid, that she recalled most of what she'd learned in his class, and that she was aware of what they were dealing with here, but she obviously couldn't.

"Now get your mask on." He pulled on his own and like Larson made several quick adjustments.

Left with no choice, she took a subtle but fairly deep breath, dragging in as much oxygen as possible. It still wasn't enough. As soon as the mask slid completely over her head, her chest went tight and her breathing became strained. Desperate to short circuit the panic attack, she inhaled slowly and pretended to check out the rest of her gear.

Breathe, Benedict. Suck it up. You'll be out of there in less than thirty friggin' minutes.

She didn't dare glance at Mark. It would take only one look at her eyes for him to figure out what was going on inside her head.

His gloved fingers closed on her right shoulder, the contact startling her more than it normally would have.

"If you can't do it, just say so. Larson and I can handle it."

He was giving her an out. As desperate as she was to take it, she couldn't afford to.

"I don't know what you're talking about." She reached for the door. He was right on her heels through the opening, but she kept going. Weak light drizzled through the windows high on the gymnasium walls, creating a grid pattern on the floor.

Sweat beaded on her forehead and her upper lip, and a small river of it ran down her rib cage, collecting at the waistline of her slacks. Without exposed skin, there was no way for her to tell if the cavernous space was cooler than the rest of the building, but she suspected it was. Livengood had initially thought the two deaths might be related to the heating repairs done on Tuesday morning, so it seemed only reasonable that he would have ordered the heat shut off to the area.

There was no door on the boys' locker room, only an arrangement of walls providing privacy, and just beyond, a room filled with lockers and benches. The attached shower room was fairly large but not particularly well lit.

Pale-yellow tiles—a washed-out Easter egg shade—covered the walls and floors and were bisected by a wide stripe of black tile that ran horizontally around the room about four feet above the floor. A dozen showerheads lined three of the walls.

As Larson looked up from where he was examining the central drain, Beth turned to check out the fourth wall where someone had used black paint and stencils to paint Go Billingham Bullets. Having managed to get her breathing somewhat under control, she tried to focus on what they were looking for.

Mark squatted opposite Larson. "Did you find something?"

As Larson shook his head, Mark got back to his feet and immediately moved to the farthest corner where he seemed to study the vent in the center of the ceiling.

Noticing Mark's interest, Larson left the drain cover off and, straightening, backed away to get a better perspective. "Looks like an air return and not a vent."

"It's recently been removed."

"There was a crew working on the heating system that morning," Larson suggested. "They could have done it."

"But why mess with a return vent if the furnace wasn't working?"

"I'll grab the ladder," Larson said.

Shifting to one side, Beth allowed Larson past her, then turned her attention back to the room. Even if she wasn't all that sure what she was looking for, there weren't that many places to search. Besides the vent overhead and the drain, the showerheads appeared to be the only other possibility.

She walked to the closest of them and peered up at it the best she could. Protective suits were not only hot and airless, even the best ones tended to distort things some and to mess with the field of vision.

Mark walked toward her. "What do you see?"

"There was a toolbox in one of the photos. As if they were planning to take something apart."

Reaching up, she tried loosening the connection between the head and the stub pipe. "I'm not a plumber, but the first thing I do when I have to work on any type of plumbing is check the water pressure."

When the showerhead didn't budge, she moved counterclockwise to the next one, immediately closing her hand around the connection, the thick neoprene gloves making it easier to get a firm, nonskid grip.

She was working on the assumption that if any of them had been removed recently, they might be only hand-tight.

"MX141 was found—" She broke off, suddenly feeling somewhat winded. After taking a deep breath, she continued. "The right pant leg of the older victim, of T. J. Duke, came into contact with heavy concentrations of MX141. If he'd turned on one of the showers without paying attention to where the head was directed, that could explain…"

She gritted her teeth as she tried the third one. *Please let* *the damn thing turn. Let me have contributed. And let me* *get the hell out of here.* But like the other two it was on tight.

Stepping past her, Mark reached for the next one in line. It turned readily in his grasp.

Chapter Seven

Mark removed the showerhead cautiously. Adrenaline had already begun to spread through him, his muscles contracting, his respiration quickening ever so slightly. He'd long ago come to accept that he was a junkie when it came to excitement, to pushing the limits.

As he started to lower the showerhead, an inch-long cylinder constructed of what looked to be some type of metal mesh dropped from inside the stub pipe.

Despite the thick gloves, he managed to catch it in his free hand. After passing the showerhead to Beth, he examined the cylinder.

The lower edges appeared to be covered in solder remnants, as if the cylinder's end had been sealed closed at one time.

What in the hell was he looking at? Some type of filtering device or an ingenious and low-tech method to deliver MX141?

Mark glanced over at Beth who was busy checking out the showerhead he'd handed her. The room hadn't offered all that many options, so he hadn't been surprised when she'd gone for the first showerhead. What had impressed him was the way she'd managed to pull herself together, effectively dealing with her personal demons when it had become crucial.

"Do you see anything that shouldn't be there?"

"There's a circular piece of screening and what looks like red neoprene or latex." She tipped the threaded connection to catch the light better. "The mesh could be legit, some kind of filter, but the bits of neoprene or latex definitely aren't."

Mark passed the cylinder to her. "What about that?"

She rolled it around on her palm for several seconds. "The construction is too crude to be manufactured." Picking it up, she held it between her index finger and thumb as she checked out the open ends. "Without using calipers to get an exact measurement, I'd say the diameter matches that of the circular screen, as if the two were originally soldered together."

Her eyes narrowed. "If it was soldered together, creating a type of miniature cage, that was then filled with a neoprene balloon loaded with MX141... When the water was turned on, the pressure alone would have been enough to rupture the neoprene."

Mark looked around as Larson returned with the ladder. "Go ahead and check out the return vent, but I think we've found what we came for."

Less than five minutes later they were changing out of the protective gear. As Mark pulled on his jacket, he glanced over and found that Beth was already dressed and Larson wasn't far behind.

"Benedict, you're with me. We'll sweep the building to be sure it's been evacuated and catch up to Livengood to get that list. Larson, locate the main shut-off valve for the water and close it. Do the same with the hot-water tank. I assume the devices weren't just planted in the boys' showers, that there are other ones that haven't been set off yet. If water gets to any of them…"

Larson nodded, his expression grim as he hurriedly swung the chair with the crime-scene tape back in front of the gymnasium doors to block them.

As all three of them hurried toward the front of the building, Mark ran down the mental list of things that needed to be handled immediately to maintain public safety.

He glanced at Larson. "When you have the water shut down, contact the Hazmat Response Unit and give them a heads-up on what we've found and pin them down on their ETA. For now you'll be working with them, collecting any additional devices."

"Got it," Larson said before leaving to locate the water valve.

Beth's cell phone went off. Without breaking stride, she jerked it from her waistband and checked the screen.

When she hesitated to answer it, he wondered if it was because he was there. "If you need to take that…"

With a slight shake of her head, she clipped the phone to her waistband again. "It can wait."

"You undoubtedly need to make a few phone calls, tell family and friends where you are."

Her only response to the statement was to adjust her jacket to cover the phone.

He actually knew very little about her personal life. Which wasn't so surprising given that less than twenty-four hours ago there'd been no reason for him to. And even now there were certain aspects he technically didn't need to be aware of, but those were the very ones that made him the most curious.

Was she currently seeing anyone?

Until the first week of July, she'd been undercover. In his experience, even if she'd been involved with someone when she'd been assigned to the Rheaume investigation, few relationships managed to survive eighteen months with little or no contact.

But what about the past four months?

There hadn't been any obvious signs at her place to suggest she'd recently hooked up with someone. No framed photos on the mantel. No extra coffee mug in the sink or toilet seat left up. Of course that didn't necessarily mean she wasn't involved. In fact, other than the old family photos hanging in her office, the place hadn't revealed much about her as a woman.

But then, his condo said even less about him. Or did it? Perhaps it was exactly the opposite. Maybe the futon in the middle of the living room where he'd slept most nights when he was home, the large coffee table loaded with terrorism reports, the fifty-two inch television and the king-size bed that only got used when he brought home a date, pretty much said everything about him.

It had been four years since his divorce, and he still hadn't gotten around to really furnishing the condo. The weekends and holidays when he had his daughters he took them to the lake cabin. Because they liked it there, and because it was the one place where he seemed to be able to block out what he did on the days when he didn't have them.

As he'd done often over the past few years, he tried to avoid adding up the days and weeks since he'd seen them last. Was it six or seven weekends now?

Looking to shift his thoughts away from his shortcomings, Mark glanced over at Beth. Her dark hair had been smooth this morning, but now curled at her temples where perspiration had dampened it. The bullet graze was also more visible. Back there in the showers, she'd surprised him. Where had a woman with a privileged upbringing, a diplomat's daughter, learned about plumbing and swinging a sledgehammer?

Maybe it was time to find out.

"Tearing out walls and taking apart plumbing. Where did that come from?"

"My grandfather was always doing something around the house. I spent a lot of time with them as I was growing up, and there wasn't much I could do when I was there, so he'd let me help him. Taught me things." She glanced over at Mark. "And then during college, I did some community work. Inner-city revitalization. Habitat for Humanity."

When her mouth tightened again and she abruptly changed the subject, he wondered if she felt she'd divulged too much about herself. And if it had been the months undercover that had made her so cautious with personal information or if, like him, it was just part of who she was.

They'd reached the administrative offices and did a quick search to be certain no one remained. They met in the hall again seconds later.

"The device we just found," Beth said as they headed for the front entrance. "Obviously it's something you haven't come across before."

"No. And I had hoped retrieving it would at least tell us if we're dealing with a foreign or domestic threat."

"But it didn't," she supplied.

"Unfortunately, no. Choosing Bellingham and not a

large city like Los Angeles or Chicago is the only break we've had so far."

There was no need to spell it out. She was already aware of the advantages of an incident occurring in a small, somewhat isolated area of the country where there were a limited number of motels and restaurants and modes of transportation. And where an outsider was more likely to be noticed. The person or people they hunted would have undoubtedly crossed paths with at least one of Bellingham's eight thousand residents.

He just needed to find that one citizen.

"The rest of the unit will arrive by two, and I'll be requesting additional agents to help with the investigation. It's unlikely that Bellingham's police station has a space large enough to handle that many. You mentioned a motel out on the highway. If they have a spa, they probably have meeting rooms. And we'll need thirty motel rooms to start with."

He'd already mapped out who would be handling which aspect of the investigation. He knew his men, knew their strengths and liked to utilize them fully. The trick was going to be finding something to keep Beth busy once she'd made all the arrangements he'd just assigned her.

"Livengood will want in on the investigation," Mark said. "And we need him. Like he said, this is his beat." He glanced over at her. "As the liaison, you'll be expected to keep him in the loop."

Seeing her shoulders tense, he knew she wasn't happy about the assignment. He hadn't expected her to be.

"Look, Benedict, you did better than I expected this morning. But both of us know you were struggling back there and that it could have gone either way. And even if that wasn't the case, even if I believed you were ready to be out in the field—which I don't—I'd have to put someone working with you."

"To protect me? Because you believe last night's shooting makes me a target?"

"Maybe it does and maybe it doesn't. But until I know for certain, you'll be working the command center. Got it?"

She didn't break stride. "Got it. But if that wasn't the case, if it turns out that Rabbit and not some terrorist hired Leon, will I still be riding a desk?"

They were still thirty-five feet from the front entrance, but, wrapping his fingers loosely around her wrist, he forced her to stop and face him. She immediately stiffened at the unexpected contact, her chin popping up and her gray eyes meeting his.

He'd planned to tell her that he was a fair man. That if it turned out she wasn't at risk, then of course he would be utilizing her in the field.

But as her dark hair slid back, exposing her throat, his thoughts derailed. His gaze followed the pale skin downward, his fingers tightening around her wrist, enough that he could feel her pulse slamming hard against the pads of his fingers. Could feel a similar throb in his own veins.

And then he was recalling the silky thing she wore beneath the heavy jacket, the way that when she'd changed out of the hazmat gear moments ago, perspiration had glued it to her rib cage and toned abdomen. To her breasts. Before he could stop himself, he was imagining what it would be like to touch her in all those places.

Suddenly remembering himself, he let her go and even stepped back half a pace, eager to put some space and sanity between them.

"Sorry," he offered. He could only imagine what she must be thinking.

Crossing her arms, she met his gaze. "I'm asking you to give me a shot. I want a chance to prove myself."

"For the record, I think Bill Monroe is full of crap."

She offered a sharp nod of understanding.

Both of them looked over as the front door suddenly opened, sunlight briefly cutting the gloom of the unlit hallway. They were too far away for Mark to tell much about the first man who stepped inside. But when he saw the television camera balanced on the shoulder of a more burly man, he realized the media had found their way around the unguarded barricades.

"Why in the hell was that door unlocked? And where's Kid Deputy?" Mark glanced down the hall, hoping to see the local cop. Or even Livengood.

Having spotted Mark and Beth, the reporter started toward them.

"How do you want to handle this?" she asked.

Mark frowned. "To be honest, the last thing I want to do right now is give a damn statement. Or play school bouncer, for that matter, but ejecting these two will be easier before a dozen of their colleagues show up. And as far as a statement is concerned, I don't see that I have much choice now. That's one bell that can't be unrung."

Reaching for his badge, he walked toward the two men. "Sir. The building is off-limits. You'll have to leave immediately."

As if he hadn't heard Mark, the reporter, dressed in dark slacks and a blue oxford shirt with the sleeves rolled back, continued to stride toward them. Without looking over his shoulder, he motioned for his cameraman to roll tape. "Is it true that the two victims didn't die of pesticide poisoning, that—"

"Sir," Mark tried again and this time held up his badge. "As a federal agent, I'm ordering you to leave this building. Now! Otherwise I'll have you arrested for impeding an investigation."

The reporter again ignored the request.

Mark was taken off guard when Beth suddenly swore. "We've got even bigger problems than these two. What if Kid Deputy didn't just wander away? What if he went looking for a restroom or a drink of water? If Larson doesn't have all the water shut off yet and the wrong faucet gets turned on…"

Mark knew she was right. That things could easily go from in-the-toilet to in-the-sewer in the next few seconds.

When Beth suddenly turned and plunged toward the closest restroom, one they'd just passed seconds earlier, he wanted to go after her, but his first priority was to protect the public. Even if they were undeserving pricks like these two.

Once he had these two out of here, he could catch up to her. She had the autoinjectors, knew how to use them. But even the chemist who'd developed the antidote had no idea just how effective it was. It had never been tested on a human being.

The reporter shoved the mike in Mark's face. "Why would the FBI get involved in the poisoning of two men?"

Barely retaining his temper, Mark sidestepped the reporter, grabbing the cameraman by the back of his sweatshirt instead and manhandling him toward the front door. It was a well-known fact that a television reporter was dead in the water unless film was rolling. "You are placing yourself in danger, sir."

He had the cameraman more than halfway to the exit when it was jerked open again. This time it was held wide as more than a dozen men and women plowed in, jostling and elbowing like a bunch of third-graders.

Not slowing and with his fingers twisting even tighter into the neck of the cameraman's sweatshirt, Mark pushed forward into the crowd, his badge held where everyone could get a good look at it.

"Listen up, people! I'm Special Agent Mark Gerritsen with the FBI. I'll have a statement for all of you shortly. If anyone prefers not to cooperate and move back outside, they will be arrested."

Most promptly turned toward the door to comply. Of course there were always a few who didn't.

Appearing at that moment, Larson grabbed one of them. "Move it!" Larson shot a look at Mark. "Where the hell is Benedict? Is she already outside?"

Mark ignored the question. "Did you get the water cut off?"

"The main valve, yes. I was on my way to take care of the hot water tank."

Mark released the man he held. "You handle this, I'll get the tank. And Benedict."

He rushed back the way she'd gone. Even with the water turned off, there might still be enough residual pressure in the lines to set off a device.

Chapter Eight

As Beth jerked open the door, Kid Deputy's unfazed gaze briefly met hers in the mirror above the sink, but then he immediately looked down and reached for the faucet handle. "You shouldn't be in here."

"Don't touch that!" But he already had, his fingers now choking the faucet handle. "If you turn on that water, we could both be killed."

His eyes popped up, meeting hers in the mirror again. He'd finally recognized that she hadn't just stumbled into the wrong bathroom. That she was there for a reason. To stop him from turning on the water.

She had the autoinjector out of her pocket and the cap off. If it happened... If he turned the handle and it set off another device, she'd inject herself first and then go after him.

But how much time did she have before she became incapacitated? Enough to reach him with the second autoinjector?

"Just let go of it," she said as calmly as she could, but even she heard the fear in her voice.

Mutely he looked down at the hand still covering the handle, almost as if it had become something foreign.

Something that shouldn't be attached to the end of his forearm. Why wasn't he releasing it?

Someone opened the door behind her. She didn't glance to see who it was. It wasn't until Mark's image was briefly reflected in the mirror next to the deputy's that she was certain who it was. The kid's color wasn't so good—his freckles more pronounced, his lips looking pale and dry in the harsh fluorescent lighting.

"It's going to be okay," she said evenly. When the kid looked over at her, she offered a confirming nod and tried flashing a smile to go with it. "Just take it easy. Just open your hand carefully."

Slowly he released the handle.

It was only then that she allowed herself to briefly focus on Mark's face in the mirror. She'd planned to play it loose, pretend that she'd been unaffected by the past few seconds, but as soon as their gazes connected in the mirror, she realized she'd never be able to pull it off. That her own coloring was nearly as bad as the kid's and that the hand holding the autoinjector was shaking. She recapped and slid the antidote into her pocket.

"You okay?" he asked quietly, taking another step into the space. Was the concern she saw on his face for the situation or for her? Or both? And what did it matter at the moment which it was?

Closing her eyes for the first time since she'd stepped into the bathroom, she took a deep breath and let it out slowly.

"Beth?"

It was only as she opened her eyes that the use of her first name really registered with her. "I'm okay." Avoiding Mark's gaze, she glanced at the kid, noticing that he hadn't moved.

"Did you get the press handled?" she asked, attempting to achieve a casualness that she still wasn't feeling.

"Larson's taking care of it."

"That's good." Reaching out, she wrapped a hand around Kid Deputy's upper arm. "Come on. Let's get you out of here."

TWENTY MINUTES after walking out of the school, Mark sat in the back of the rental SUV. Even though Livengood's men had cleared the school grounds of media, the reporters hadn't gone far and were now camped out on the road.

Waiting for him.

Mark scanned the carefully worded and brief statement again. The media wasn't going to find it particularly satisfactory, but that really wasn't his goal at the moment.

For now he just needed to give them something, and at the same time soft-sell the situation. Not because he felt comfortable with that approach, but because those were his orders. And because, as much as he didn't like misleading the public, it was probably in their best interest.

With no idea who they were dealing with, whether it was a domestic or foreign threat, there was no way to make even an educated guess about the next possible target. Or if the same delivery method would be used. So what in the hell good would it do to warn people about a danger that they couldn't hope to protect themselves against? How could you tell a whole nation that simply turning on a faucet could kill them?

Feeling completely exhausted and at the same time frustrated, he ran a hand over his face, trying to clear those thoughts from his mind. What he needed right now was a cup of strong coffee and to have the next fifteen minutes behind him. Once he'd made the statement, he could get back to the more important work—hunting down the people who had done this.

Looking through the windshield, he spotted both Larson and Beth. Larson was talking with two of Livengood's officers, and Beth was still on her cell phone, probably making motel and meeting-space arrangements.

As he watched, she paced to the edge of the parking lot, her stride somewhat aggressive, but he couldn't find fault with the way her ass moved. Or the way he liked watching it.

Back there in the bathroom, he'd called her by her first name. So, when was it that he'd stopped thinking of her as Benedict? Stopped seeing her strictly as another member of the unit?

Mark rubbed his forehead. It couldn't happen again. If she was to be accepted by the other agents in the unit, he couldn't afford to treat her any differently. Despite the fact that in two very key ways she was different from the rest of them. She was female and someone had tried to kill her seventeen hours ago.

And as bad as it sounded, he needed to pray that they'd try again.

Because in the long run, even though it put her at risk, it might possibly save countless lives.

Acceptable casualties. He wondered who'd coined the friggin' phrase. It damn sure hadn't been someone with a gun leveled at his head. Or the head of someone he cared about.

There were aspects of his job that he truly despised. And what he was about to do to Beth—pinning a bull's-eye to her chest—was definitely one of them.

Showtime, he thought with harsh resignation. As he

climbed out, he grabbed his suit jacket and pulled it on. Beth ended the phone call and, turning back, spotted him.

The wind had picked up enough that it now harvested the last of the fall foliage, sending those leaves and the ones already on the ground rushing past her and toward the front of the school.

Clipping the phone to her waistband, she headed back toward him. When she was close enough, she said, "The motel is in the midst of renovations, so all I could reserve were nineteen rooms. No problem with the meeting space, though. Or with providing food."

He started to replace the tie he'd taken off earlier, then decided against it and tossed it into the back seat instead. "We'll still need more rooms. See if there is anything close by."

"Already did. There's a bed-and-breakfast almost across the street and one a few miles down the road. They're holding whatever rooms they have available and they're willing to accept a discounted rate, but there's a three-night minimum and I couldn't get them to budge."

"That's not a problem. At least some of us will be here longer than that." He glanced down at the speech a final time before pitching the pad onto the back seat with the tie. He wanted to keep it relaxed and flowing, make the press believe that they didn't have a lot of answers yet.

"Come on, Benedict," he said, and motioned with his head. "My job is to give them a white-bread version of what happened here, and yours is to be as conspicuous as possible standing next to me."

IN A MATTER OF HOURS the motel meeting room had morphed into a command center for Mark's eleven-member team and the seventeen additional agents who had arrived since this morning. Because the recently remodeled space smelled heavily of fresh paint and new carpet, a pair of exterior doors leading to the unfinished pool deck had been propped open.

As the night had cooled down into the forties, so had the room. Which wasn't a bad thing since the frigid temperature along with an overload of caffeine were at least partly responsible for keeping them all functioning.

It was after 10:30 p.m. when Mark placed his laptop on the table closest to the open doors. He'd just come from a meeting with the medical examiner, the last in a long line of interviews.

After shedding his coat, he dropped into a chair and flicked on the computer. As he waited for it to boot up, he caught sight of Beth standing next to a table across the room and in deep conversation with Travis Mickels and Scott Duzenberry, both his agents, and Jenny Springer, a veteran agent and an information bloodhound on loan from the Atlanta field office. He'd worked with Springer before, had always found her to be both competent and diligent.

Even though he'd had to be in and out all day, he hadn't been overly concerned about Beth's safety. As long as she was surrounded by three or four agents, he didn't expect the unsub to go after her. He still had asked Jenny Springer to keep an eye on Beth, though. To make sure that she was never left alone.

When he'd asked about Beth's investigative skills, Jenny had been reasonably complimentary—which for Jenny was highly unusual. Given Jenny's remarks and the way Beth had handled herself at the school this morning and during the noon press statement, he wondered if somewhere along the line she had stepped on the wrong toes. Either Bill Monroe's or the toes of someone even higher up the food chain. She wouldn't be the first agent to find herself in that position. Or once in it, the target of an unfair and unjustified witch hunt.

So, what was he going to do if he found out that was the case? Was he going to stand by and do nothing? Or get involved and in the process place his own career on the line?

Almost as if she'd felt that she was being watched, Beth's eyes lifted, connecting with his. Maybe it was only the lighting, but she looked tired. She couldn't have gotten much sleep last night and today had been a tough one for all of them. And on top of that, she was having to cope with the reassignment and suddenly finding herself a possible target. All in all, given the pressure, though, she appeared to be holding up okay.

She suddenly broke eye contact and, stepping back half a step from the group, grabbed her cell phone and twisted away. As she had earlier in the day, she checked the screen and then reclipped it unanswered to her waist.

Was it the same caller?

As she rejoined the group, she shot a glance across the room, but avoided his gaze. He got the impression that it was intentional, that she was ducking him for some reason, but he couldn't imagine why. But then, maybe he was reading too much into absolutely nothing.

Mark refocused his attention to the computer screen and the reports he needed to compose.

When his cell phone went off several seconds later, he didn't hesitate to answer.

"Special Agent Gerritsen, this is Geoffrey Benedict." The booming voice on the other end wasn't a familiar one but the name certainly was. Why would Beth's father be calling him?

"Yes, sir, Mr. Benedict. What can I do for you?"

"I'm sorry to disturb you, especially at this time of night, but I've been trying to get in touch with my daughter. I understand from Bill Monroe that she's been reassigned and is now working with you."

"Yes, sir. As of this morning." Mark split his attention between the phone call and the computer screen. "Have you tried calling her cell phone?"

"Yes. I've left messages."

Were those the phone calls that she hadn't taken, then? But why wouldn't she want to talk to her father?

"She's been quite busy," Mark supplied. "We all have been. Is there some kind of emergency, sir?"

Geoffrey Benedict cleared his throat. "No. I don't suppose it's an emergency." The retired diplomat's voice faded some, sounding older and maybe a little less certain. "Bill assured me that he had made sure you were aware of my daughter's current situation."

"Mr. Benedict, as I said before, we're in the midst of an investigation."

"Could you at least tell me how long she'll be reassigned there with you?"

"You'll need to take that up with her, sir. I'm sure if you've left messages, she'll contact you as soon as possible."

The silence was especially heavy this time as Mark waited, and then, "Is there any possibility that I might speak with her now? I mean, if she's there with you?"

Mark glanced to where Beth and the rest of the group clustered around a computer screen, discussing some aspect of the investigation. If she hadn't returned the calls, there was undoubtedly a reason, and Mark had no right to intrude into her personal life.

"No, sir. I'm sorry. She isn't available. But I'll make sure she gets your message."

He was still frowning when Larson found him several minutes later.

Because Larson had nearly as much experience with counterterrorism as Mark, he always made a point of reviewing developments with him. They'd talked several times over the past nine hours, but it was the first time they'd been in the same room together since this morning.

"So, what's the status?" Mark asked.

Larson grabbed a chair and sat, placing his coffee cup on the table. "The Hazmat Response Unit has checked every bit of the plumbing, and they'll be starting the room-by-room search in the morning, but so far they've found only one additional device and it was in the boys' shower room."

Why just the boys' shower room? Why not the girls', too? Because there was some kind of interruption?

"The time frame for when the chemical could have been placed has been narrowed some," Mark said, "to between 10:00 p.m. on Monday night and Tuesday night when our vics showed up. Which still leaves a sizable window of opportunity."

Mark ran a hand through his hair. "The heating repair crew has been interviewed. Not one of them saw anything unusual. Springer and Beth are running more-detailed background checks on them and on the school faculty. Maybe they'll turn up a connection with an extremist group."

"So you think it's more likely a domestic situation and not a foreign one?" Larson asked.

"I'm not eliminating anything, but it seems to be

shaping up that way. After nearly a hundred interviews, we've got nothing. No eyewitness that can put a stranger in that school or anywhere else in town. So either our unsub is able to blend in or he's local."

After four months and two more deaths, it didn't feel as if they'd gained much ground. And in the back of his head, he couldn't ignore the similarities to another case. It had been nearly seven years since the first anthrax-tainted letter arrived in Florida. After countless man hours and a multi-agency investigation, no arrest had been made. And while the investigation was ongoing, there were fewer agents working it now.

Mark booted down the computer. "We've pretty well covered local businesses and have moved on to the charge slips on self-service gas pumps, but I bet we won't find anything there, either." He was beat. All of his people were quickly becoming that way. He couldn't afford for them to burn out too soon.

"There's not much more to be done tonight," Mark said. "Maybe you should get some sleep."

As Larson got to his feet slowly, he motioned with his head. "How's Benedict doing?"

"Fine." Mark had noticed Larson watching her closely several times.

"So no fallout from the press statement? No attempts to get to her?"

"No. But then, she's been under constant surveillance. Not exactly an easy target to hit."

"And whose watchful eyes will be on her tonight?" Larson asked, but it was plain in his tone that he already knew.

"She's my responsibility," Mark said. "So she's in the room next to mine."

Larson's mouth tightened, but he obviously knew enough not to say what he was thinking.

As Larson left, Mark grabbed a cup of coffee and walked outside to clear his head. Even though the pool appeared to be mostly complete, bright-orange mesh fencing kept people from getting too close.

Several large pines stood between the pool and the building, the breeze sighing in their branches. Keeping to their shadows, Mark wandered twenty-feet from the door before turning and checking out the lit interior. The room was still filled with agents, Beth among them, but one or two agents were beginning to gather up their laptops and briefcases, exchanging good-nights. Possibly making plans to meet for breakfast. A few would hook up for drinks in someone's room before turning in. Perhaps catch the end of a televised basketball game.

As he was watching, Beth turned to Scott Duzenberry and first said something and then smiled. At least some members of the team seemed to be accepting her well enough. Mark knew what Larson had wanted to say. That Mark shouldn't feel any more responsible for Beth than he did for any other agent assigned to the unit. Nineteen months ago, when Nidia Turner had been killed, he'd blamed himself. Still blamed himself for sending her into the situation that day.

When his phone went off, he unclipped it, but this time checked the caller ID. Even when he recognized his ex-wife's phone number, he debated taking the call. But he did. Because in the back of his mind he was always worried that something had happened to one of his daughters, to Gracie or Addison.

"Hi."

There was a pause on the other end, long enough that Mark started to grow uneasy. After setting the cup of coffee down on the window ledge in front of him, he turned his back to the window. "Is everything okay, Traci?"

"Yeah." She sounded tired or worried. He couldn't tell which. Her moods weren't really his responsibility anymore, but some habits were harder than others to break. "I just needed to know what time you were going to pick up the girls tomorrow."

He ran a hand through his hair. "Look, Traci. I'm not going to be able to make it."

There was a longer silence this time. "I can't believe you're doing this to the girls again. Not after what Gracie went through the last time."

"I'm sorry. Obviously it can't be helped."

"It never can be. Have you noticed that?" Her sharp exhale buffeted the receiver. "They're your children, Mark. It wasn't immaculate conception. You were there when they were conceived. And even managed to be there when they were born. But sometimes it feels as if that was the last time you were there for any of us."

It was an old argument. And tonight of all nights he wasn't up to going over it yet again. "The divorce was your decision, Traci. Not mine."

"You left us long before I ever contacted the attorney."

"I had a job to do."

"And you had a family, too."

"I know," he said quietly. "Do you want me to talk to Gracie? Maybe if she heard it from me it would be easier."

"No. I'd rather not tell her tonight. She's got a test in the morning, and I don't want her thinking about…"

"What if I call back tomorrow? About the time I would

normally be picking them up? I can explain. Maybe that way she wouldn't worry so much."

"Don't bother. I'll tell her when I pick her up," Traci said, anger creeping into her tone again.

"It's not a bother. And I think it might help her—"

"Having you around more often is what would help her. Not getting a phone call telling her why you can't show up. Again."

"Look. Just because I can't be there doesn't mean I'm not concerned."

She'd never been able to understand that the job he did, he did partly for his girls. Because he wanted them to feel safe at night and not afraid. Because he didn't want their futures to include another 9/11. All she'd ever been able to see is that it took him away from them.

"Do you have plans?" he asked, calmly. "Do you want me to call my dad? See if he can keep them?"

"I don't think that's a good idea."

The words and even the tone of her voice struck an uncomfortable chord within him. Traci had often dropped the girls off at his dad's. What was different about this time? Had something happened recently while they were there? Had his father forgotten about Gracie's peanut allergy?

Or was Traci just trying to make things harder on him?

"Why wouldn't it be a good idea?"

Traci lowered her voice. "It's not something I want to discuss over the phone, or in front of the girls. They're just in the other room and could walk in at any moment."

Which meant she was calling from the bedroom and could easily close the door, but he knew not to make the suggestion.

What in the hell was going on? He and Traci had talked

earlier in the week and everything had been okay. She hadn't mentioned any problems with his dad.

"When do you want to talk about it, then?" He was finding it difficult to keep his growing frustration under wraps and knew it came through in his voice.

"When do I want to talk about it? Never! So maybe you should call your attorney and let him fill you in."

"I'd rather talk to—"

She disconnected.

"You," he finished.

He started to hit the recall button, but knew it would be a waste of time. Traci wouldn't answer. That's how she'd handled most things during their marriage and the habit had only become more pronounced recently. She'd drop a bomb and then make herself unavailable.

He inhaled sharply and turned to check out the command center again. Only a few agents remained and most of those were packing it in, too.

Mark rubbed his jaw. What in the hell had she meant about contacting his attorney? What could she want? He was already giving her double the amount of child support that he was required to pay, and since the divorce, he'd periodically bailed her out when she'd gotten herself in trouble with credit cards, so it couldn't be about the money. Which left what? Visitation? Is that what she was going after? Nearly a year ago she'd threatened to take him back to court. To ask for sole custody.

His gut tightened. Not his girls. Traci could have anything of his that she wanted, his retirement, what was left of his savings account. Anything but sole custody.

Some sound behind him made him realize that he was no longer alone. Turning, he sensed more than saw someone standing in the shadows beneath the trees. He realized it was Beth.

Obviously, she'd used another exit, and more than likely had overheard at least part of his conversation with Traci, so there was no reason to pretend otherwise. "I have two daughters, nine and eleven. Gracie and Addison."

She cocked her head to the side, as if she were studying him. He realized it was something she did often.

"And this is your weekend to have them," she said simply. "And for obvious reasons you can't be there." She crossed her arms in front of her, the bottled water she held half-empty and dangling from the fingers of her left hand.

"Yeah." He put his phone away. "Everyone is calling tonight, it seems."

Her eyes narrowed. "What do you mean?"

"Your father called a few minutes ago. He's been trying to reach you."

"So when he couldn't, he phones you." Her mouth tightened and then she looked away for several seconds. She lifted the water to her lips and took a hurried sip. "Perfect."

The tone of her voice made it clear that she considered it anything but perfect.

"I told him that I'd see that you got the message."

"And now you have. I'm sorry. I'll make sure he doesn't call you again in the future."

"It's fine," he assured.

"No. It's not."

She looked more upset than the situation warranted. After all, it was just a phone call.

"Want to talk about it?" he asked.

"Not any more than you want to talk about what went wrong in your marriage."

Touché.

She took another swig of water. "I also got a call a little bit ago. An interesting one."

"From?"

"A detective with Baltimore PD. They've identified the connection between Rabbit Rheaume and Leon Tyber, including a paper trail."

"So I was wrong. You're not a target." The news didn't strike him as he'd expected it to. He found himself more relieved than upset.

But what about Beth? Had her reaction to the detective's call been the exact opposite? Had she been more upset than relieved? Did she find being a terrorist's target easier to face than possibly finding herself under Bill Monroe's control again?

Mark could ask her, he supposed, but he already knew that she wouldn't answer. Just as she'd refused to discuss her father's call.

"And you're wondering if, because you're no longer bait, I'll be sending you back to Baltimore?"

Chapter Nine

"Yes." The water bottle crackled as Beth's fingers choked it too tightly, the sound setting her nerves even more on edge. Loosening her hold, she tried to block out just how much rode on Mark's answer.

From the moment she'd stepped off the plane this morning, she'd been desperately trying to make herself an asset, a task made more difficult by the assignments she'd been given—making motel reservations and arranging meeting space; running background checks on teachers and hardworking trades people; running a list of names supplied by agents out in the field against a variety of federal databases. It was busy work. The kind that could be done by anyone. The type that wouldn't be enough to guarantee a permanent spot with the unit.

She fought to control her growing frustration. Not just with her situation, but with her father, too. Maybe she should consider herself lucky that he'd only asked for a message to be relayed. That he hadn't decided to fill in Mark the same way he'd filled in Bill Monroe.

She'd been so focused on her own thoughts that it wasn't until Mark moved toward her, stepping into the shade beneath the tree, that she realized she still stood mostly in the shadows.

"Tell me, Beth. I'm curious." He leaned toward her, his voice dropping. Not quite a whisper but low enough to give the illusion of intimacy. "How long did you think about just keeping the detective's call to yourself?"

He'd intentionally invaded her space, his crisp, white shirt only inches from her nose. As she took a shallow breath, it wasn't just the scent of his cologne that reached her, but that of laundry starch and warm male skin.

"I'll admit to being human," she said. "To wanting to make the transfer permanent." She met his gaze. "So. Should I be packing my bags?"

"Not tonight," Mark said simply as he shifted backward half a step.

Not tonight? It wasn't much of an answer. There wasn't a whisper of a promise in it, but she still felt as if she'd dodged a bullet. At least temporarily.

There was an awkward half second when both of them seemed to be waiting for the other to say good night.

It was Mark who made the first move, walking to where he'd left his coffee on the window ledge. "Since it was Rabbit who hired the hit and he's now dead, there's no longer any reason to worry about your safety, is there?"

"No."

"Good night, then," he said as he dumped the coffee on the ground.

"Yeah," she said. "Good night."

As she watched him walk away, she admitted that not wanting to be attracted to him and not being that way were two entirely different things. Every time he was within a few feet of her, every time that sizzle of awareness flooded her system, she lost track of everything else.

Especially her resolve to keep her distance.

HOURS LATER the phone next to the bed awakened her from what felt like a drug-induced coma. She groped for it, undecided about whether, when she finally found the phone, she was going to answer it or hurl it across the room.

Who in the hell would be calling at this time of night? And then as her head cleared some, she thought she knew.

Her father.

If he could get Mark's number, finding out where she was staying would be easy by comparison. And her father was nothing if not persistent. And as far as taking *no* gracefully, well, it just didn't happen. Stubbornness and determination were two things she and her father had in common.

Sitting on the edge of the bed and still in the dark, Beth dragged the phone toward her. As it rang again, she picked up the receiver, uncertain what she was going to say to her father once they got past the prerequisite hello.

"Is this Beth Benedict?"

She didn't recognize the male voice, but assumed it belonged to someone on the motel staff or to one of the other agents. "This is she," she mumbled.

"Your voice. I like it. Is it always that husky?" As he made the last statement, his had dropped.

Originally relieved when she realized the caller wasn't her father, adrenaline now hit her system. "Who is this?"

"Let's just say that when I saw you on television today, I became an admirer of sorts." She could hear piano music in the background. "How's your room there at the Laurel-wood Inn and Spa? Did they get rid of the bedbugs?"

The wording of his last question pretty much did away with the possibility that the caller was any type of motel employee. A crank call, then? But how had they gotten her name? Her room number?

"It's a little late for a survey, so I'm hanging up now."

"I wouldn't do that."

Something in his tone kept her on the line. "Why not?"

"Because I'm the reason you're here in Bellingham."

It was as if someone had slapped her hard across the face, finally doing away with the last traces of sleep. The reason she was here in Bellingham? There were a lot of nutcases out there. Even during the short course of their investigation, it wouldn't be unusual for several to have been unearthed. But was this one of them?

"You don't believe me, do you?" There was obvious amusement in his voice.

"I didn't say that," she said cautiously, trying to plot the best course, the right questions to ask.

"But you were thinking it. You were trying to figure out if I'm for real."

"Why not convince me, then?" She turned on the lamp, squinting against the sudden glare. "If you are who you say you are, it shouldn't be difficult."

"Because that's not the reason I called, and because you'll have all the proof you need soon enough."

"What exactly does that mean?"

"That I'm not done in Bellingham." Something in his voice, the confidence coupled with the choice of words sent a chill through her and persuaded her that he wasn't some harmless creep. That there was a good possibility he was the real deal.

But why call her instead of the lead investigator? What was he after?

"What kind of proof am I going to have?" she asked. Keeping him on the line forever wasn't going to help. Not unless the call was traced. But for that to happen, she needed help.

Mark had contacted her several times during the day. His cell number would be stored on the incoming call log. But where in the hell had she left her cell phone? Her purse?

"What kind of proof?" There was more amusement in his voice now.

She'd briefly lost track of the conversation. Something she couldn't afford to do if she wanted to keep him on the phone. "That was my question."

She anxiously scanned the room for her handbag. Where in the hell had she left it?

"Why the undeniable kind of proof, of course. You're sounding a little breathless. I hope I haven't upset you."

"No." She didn't need anyone to tell her that she wasn't really equipped to handle this call. That there were people far better trained at this type of thing. No doubt Mark was one of them.

She spotted the purse on the dresser. By grabbing the base of the motel phone in one hand and taking it with her, she was able to stretch just far enough to reach the strap. She jerked the bag off the dresser, the contents spilling on to the carpet. After seizing her cell phone, she retreated to the bed again and immediately went to the incoming log.

Even as she keyed in the text message to Mark, she needed to continue asking questions. Draw out the conversation and keep the caller on the line as long as possible.

He'd called to tell her something. So maybe the key was not to let him get to it too soon.

If she could force him slightly off topic, without actually pissing him off and having him hang up on her, she might buy some time. "Is it true, what they say? That television adds ten pounds?"

He gave a fast chuckle. "You're wondering if maybe I saw you somewhere besides TV, whether our paths crossed today. You're quick. I like that. It'll make the game more interesting."

Why hadn't he answered her question? Because their paths had crossed?

She hit the Send key. "What game?"

"The one we're going to play, you and me. Just to make the roadtrip interesting."

"What makes you think I'll play along?" she asked, her gaze cemented to the lighted screen of her cell phone. *Come on, Mark.*

"Because if you don't, lots of people will die."

Beth climbed to her feet, the tightness in her chest increasing. "And if I do, they won't?"

When the soft knock on her room door came, she was already in front of it. She flipped off the security latch and the night bolt, the sound of the latter louder than she would have liked. But at that moment she would have been willing to tear down the door with her bare hands just not to be alone.

"No. That's not how the game works."

"Then maybe you should tell me how it does work. I mean if you expect me to play."

"People are going to die either way."

Beth moved backward, allowing Mark to step inside, but

she only gave him a cursory look, her attention completely focused on the caller.

"So if people are going to die, no matter what I do," she canted the receiver away from her ear, enough that Mark could listen. "Why should I play?"

"Because if you play well enough, I might just let *you* live."

Chapter Ten

Mark took the phone receiver out of her stiff fingers as soon as the call was disconnected. "You okay?" he asked. He was watching her closely.

"Sure. I'm fine."

Snugging her arms in front of her, she tried to pretend she felt calm. "He just took me by surprise."

Only hours ago she'd believed that she *wasn't* being hunted by terrorists and now… Beth uncrossed her arms. "What time is it, anyway?"

"Just after four."

He dropped the phone receiver back onto the base and pulled out the desk chair. "I need you to write down everything that was said and in as much detail as possible. Don't leave anything out. Include any thoughts you may have had at the time. Anything and everything, you understand?"

"Sure." She sat and picked up the pen supplied by the motel and the small notebook she'd left on the desk. As she started putting words to paper, though, the choppy handwriting didn't look like hers. Because it was so scratchy and difficult to read, by the time she flipped to the second page, she'd finally given up and switched to block letters.

She knew it wasn't fear making her hand shake, that it was just the adrenaline, but would Mark know that? Or would he see the unsteady handwriting as a sign of weakness?

It was only as she jotted down the last few exchanges that she realized just how short the conversation had been. Probably no more than two or three minutes, but at the time it had seemed much longer.

She ripped off the four pages and passed them. "I'm afraid there's not much there."

Because the bed provided the only other seating in the cramped room, he sat on the edge of it, facing her. He'd pulled on pants but hadn't bothered with a shirt.

She could barely recall the last time a half-dressed man sat on the edge of her bed. During the eighteen months undercover, she'd avoided anyone from her previous life— for their protection and for her own.

And during the four months since the investigation had ended, she'd been screwed up just enough that she'd been leery of letting anyone get too close. In the end, having grown tired of being scared, and feeling so damn alone, she'd gone home to Virginia. To the family estate with all the high-tech security. To the only family she had left.

To the one person who should have been loyal to her. Her father.

But he hadn't been.

Taking a shallow breath, Beth pushed the thought aside. Right now there was something much bigger on her plate that needed her attention.

When she shifted her focus back to Mark, he was frowning. "Sorry about the writing."

"No problem." He continued studying the pages, and, because she wanted to avoid thinking about both the caller and her father, she watched Mark, ostensibly to offer answers if he had any questions.

A new-growth beard shadowed his jaw. On some men, the I-need-to-shave look suggested late-night bars and too much drinking. On Mark, the shadowed jaw when coupled with bare chest and bare feet, with rumpled hair and rumpled sheets, looked a whole lot more danger-ous… It evoked images of another type of bingeing. The sexual kind.

The room's heat shut off. When chill-bumps immedi-ately broke out on her arms, they were enough to remind her that she wasn't exactly dressed for company. White boxers and a T-shirt might technically cover her body, but because the material was on the thin side, they weren't exactly concealing.

Not that he seemed to have noticed.

Mark glanced up at that moment. "He made no attempt to disguise his voice. I assume because he's not concerned about you recognizing it?"

"And I didn't."

"So there's no chance that this is the same caller who contacted Rheaume in July? The phone call you thought might be connected to MX141?"

"And the voice I thought I would recognize if I heard it again? No. This guy sounds as if he might have either been raised in the Midwest or spent a considerable amount of time there."

When he glanced at her quizzically, she explained, "He speaks with what's called a lower vowel back merger. He loses a vowel when he says certain words."

Nodding, Mark glanced down at the pages again. "He makes no attempt to justify his actions. There's no mention of a grievance or some type of cause. But he refers to bedbugs?"

The area between Mark's dark brows puckered. "It's an odd question to ask. Maybe it wasn't a random one. Maybe he's trying to tell us that he stayed here at some point in the past or lived in the area and knew the motel had a reputation."

Getting to his feet, he paced to the center of the room. "How did he act when you said you were hanging up?"

"As if he wanted to be sure I didn't."

"But not desperate?"

"No. Not desperate," she agreed. "Confident was more like it. He knew what it would take to keep me on the phone." Recalling the chilling effects of his words, Beth folded her arms in front of her again.

"And yet there's nothing here to suggest that he'd done any homework on you. That he knew anything more than your name. If he had, I don't think he could have resisted using it."

"Why do you think that?"

"He does everything he can to keep you off balance. He wants to be in control." Mark ran a hand through his short, dark hair. "When you tried to change the course of the conversation by asking about the camera adding pounds, he never actually responds to your question. Instead he takes back control by hitting you with the game he wants to play and with people dying."

He was frowning again. "He needs someone to appreciate his cleverness, what he does. And he's chosen you. Because he saw you this afternoon." Mark's eyes narrowed. "Because I made it impossible for him not to—"

"He says he isn't through in Bellingham," she said solemnly.

"I suspect he is and just wants us to believe if we hurry

we can save lives here. But it's more likely, if there are additional victims, they're already dead. The 911 call just hasn't gone out yet."

She'd been sitting, but now climbed to her feet. What was he suggesting? "So we're going to do nothing?"

"No. We do what we've been doing from the start. We do everything we can."

AS MARK STEPPED out of the rental SUV four hours later, he scanned the area surrounding the white clapboard farmhouse.

He'd received Livengood's call only a short time ago, but five local PD cars as well as one of the Hazmat Response Units and Larson's car were already in front. Not seeing Larson, Mark assumed he was inside. Walking the scene. Gathering evidence.

Counting the dead.

Every man drew some satisfaction from being good at his chosen profession. From reaching a level of proficiency. But there were moments when Mark would have liked to be proven wrong, and this was one of them.

The weather was probably typical for the area, overcast and with temperature in the low forties.

He glanced across the roof of the SUV as Beth got out the other side. "Nice place."

"Pretty," she agreed. "And remote." Turning, she seemed to briefly study the tree-covered mountain behind the farmhouse.

She'd managed to tame her dark hair again, smoothing it so that it hung sleekly. She wore trim-fitting slacks and a black blazer now, but as much as he might want to block out the image of her sitting at the desk a few hours ago in a thin T-shirt and boxer shorts, he couldn't. Nor could he recall the last time he'd wanted to touch a woman quite as much as he wanted to touch her.

Three years ago, when he'd been her instructor at Quantico, he'd known she was beautiful, proficient with a firearm and intelligent. In short, she'd impressed him more than any other new recruit he'd taught. But in the past thirty-six hours he'd learned several more things about her—that she was strong and courageous.

And because of him, she was in extreme danger.

His gut tightened in remorse. But what was done was done, and no matter how much he wanted to send her someplace safe, he wouldn't. Because as long as she was with him, there was an outside chance this madman could be stopped. And because he suspected even if he tried to send her away, she wouldn't go.

As she suddenly faced him, he forced his attention off her and onto the property again.

Besides the large home, there were three outbuildings: a barn, a lean-to with two tractors parked beneath it, and a chicken coop. All of them had been built on the downslope to ensure that groundwater runoff from livestock didn't contaminate the drinking well.

The only livestock he saw, though, were some free-range chickens and a small herd of cattle clustered beneath a large oak in a nearby pasture.

She closed the car door. "Seems like an odd target for a terrorist, doesn't it?"

"You're right. He's not acting like a terrorist. He's acting more like a spree killer. One with the most deadly weapons at his disposal, capable of easily taking out thousands. But he doesn't."

Which didn't mean he wouldn't. That Bellingham

wasn't what Mark had originally labeled it—a warm-up exercise. Maybe the more telling questions that needed to be answered were why the school, why only the boys' shower room, why those who lay dead in this farmhouse. How were they connected to each other?

If they knew why, they'd stand a better chance of learning who.

As he rounded the front end of the car, another SUV pulled in behind, loaded with two more agents. Mark continued toward the house where he saw Livengood and his deputies waiting on the large wrap-around front porch. Beth fell in beside him. As they passed a group of chickens scrabbling at the ground, she paused, so he did, too.

"They're Rhode Island reds," he supplied.

"They're beautiful."

"Maybe, but you might want to be careful around them."

Looking up, she appeared surprised. "Why?"

"Because they're territorial as hell." At her questioning look, he added, "I spent the first fifteen years of my life on a farm."

Continuing toward the house, he lengthened his stride, wondering why he'd shared that piece of information with her. As he climbed the front steps, he checked out the somber faces of the waiting deputies and Livengood.

"What can you tell me so far?" Mark asked as he hit the top tread.

Looking down at his feet briefly, Livengood smoothed the rim of the hat he held. "Names are Richard and Sally Ravenel and their seventeen-year-old son Kenny. Found them in the upstairs bathroom."

Mark could hear the shock in the police chief's voice. "How'd you find them?"

"A 911 call."

"Who phoned it in?" Beth asked as she reached the porch and stood beside Mark.

"The call came from here. It was a man's voice, but he wouldn't give his name and hung up fast." Livengood continued to manipulate the hat rim.

In a place like Bellingham, a neighbor wouldn't hesitate to identify himself. Out of the corner of his eye, seeing Beth's mouth tighten, he suspected that she'd come to the same conclusion he had. That the 911 caller had been the same man who'd phoned her at 4:00 a.m.

"I'll need a tape of the call," Mark said.

"Sure." Livengood nodded. "I'll see that you get it right away."

Even if the call had been placed on the home phone, because of the MX141 that had been used, it was unlikely the caller would have done it from inside the house.

Mark motioned toward the barn. "Is there a telephone out there?"

"Maybe." Livengood's eyes narrowed suddenly and he glanced over at his deputies. "Anyone seen or heard Max?"

"Who is Max?" Beth asked.

"Richard's dog. A shepherd mix. Big thing, but harmless. He's usually locked up in the barn at night. With all this commotion he should be going crazy by now."

Mark assigned the task of checking the barn for a phone and locating the family dog to the agents in the second car, then returned his attention to the police chief. "So tell me about the Ravenels."

"Up until three years ago, when Richard remarried and moved out here with Sally, he was the coach down at the high school."

"Any other children?" Mark asked.

"Kenny was actually Sally's son. Richard had a daughter. She died about nine years ago. A hunting accident."

"Where are Kenny's father and the first Mrs. Ravenel?"

"Dead. She died in an auto accident and Kenny's dad had cancer."

Livengood tossed his hat onto the seat of the rocking chair behind him and used both hands to wipe his eyes. He immediately looked away, tightening his jaw in an effort to stem his emotions.

Mark didn't need to be told that there was more to the story—there always was. But early in his career he'd discovered that knowing too many personal and inconsequential details about the dead not only made it harder to sleep, it also made it more difficult to do his job.

After giving Livengood a few seconds to collect himself, Mark continued, "Can you think of anyone who might want them dead? Anyone who Richard, Sally or Kenny had a run-in with?"

"Recently? Not that I know of. There might be a few who remember Richard from his years of coaching, though."

"Meaning what?" Mark asked.

"He was ex-military and tended to work his kids pretty hard. Most of them respected him for it, but a few didn't."

"Any names come to mind?"

"No. But I'll check with the principal and do some asking around." Livengood looked like a man who'd been knocked down one too many times over the past few days. "You think it's possible this guy is local?"

"I think it's a possibility. Any idea if the Laurelwood Inn ever had a problem with bedbugs?"

If the question surprised the police chief, he didn't show

it. "Maybe in the past. Place was pretty bad at one time, but it's been cleaned up for five or six years now."

Mark filed the information away, uncertain where it fit into the puzzle. Had Beth's caller used the bedbug question to mislead them, to convince them that he was either local or had lived in the area at some time?

At that moment the first body bag appeared. Livengood and his men shuffled backward, watching in grim silence as the bag was carried past the large baskets of orange flowers on either side of the door and then down the wooden steps.

Beth had followed Mark to the railing and now stood next to him.

As the body bag disappeared into the back of the waiting vehicle, his gut tightened. Had it been the seventeen-year-old kid with his whole life ahead him? Or had it been one of the parents who'd rushed to help their son?

Instead of turning back to watch the remaining two Ravenels carried out, Mark stared at the rolling farmland, wondering how many more porches he'd have to stand on, how many more people would die before it was over.

No one spoke until the third and last Ravenel had been slid into the back of a waiting vehicle.

Larson emerged right behind the bleak procession, stripping off his mask and gloves as he stepped out into the fresh air.

"Same type of dispersal device. Looks as if the son went in to take a shower and the parents came running when they realized something was wrong."

"Fingerprints?" Mark asked.

"Not on the showerhead. We'll collect what we can from other surfaces."

"Were you able to narrow down the time frame?"

"There are hamburger patties made up on a plate next to the sink. Looks as if they've been there a day or two."

Livengood shifted forward. "My deputies made some calls. Last time anyone heard from any of the Ravenels was Thursday afternoon."

"Timing sounds about right," Larson said.

So if the family had been dead since Thursday, why hold off on the emergency call? Because he'd expected them to be found before now? Because he'd grown tired of waiting? Something didn't quite add up.

"Any signs of forced entry?" Beth asked.

Her question had been directed at Larson, but it was Livengood who answered. "There's a basement entrance around back. It wasn't locked when my deputy arrived."

"Would you consider that unusual?" Beth asked.

"No. Folks around here aren't always so cautious, and having a dog sometimes makes them even less so."

Mark's phone rang. Glancing down, he recognized the cell number of one of the agents he'd sent down to the barn. "What did you find?"

"Dog's been shot. The phone is the cordless variety and the handset is missing. There's another structure with some tractors just below this one. We're going to head down and check it out."

Mark dropped the cell phone back into his pocket.

When he looked around, Beth had walked to the farthest corner of the porch and seemed to be studying the steep incline behind the house. It was the second time she'd shown more than casual interest. Did she see something?

Taking several quick steps back from the rail, she then hurried the length of the covered side porch.

By the time he reached her, she stood at the back railing. "What's going on?"

"There's someone watching us from up there," she tossed back as she jumped over the rail.

Mark vaulted after her. As soon as his feet hit the hard-packed red clay, he reached for his weapon.

Within three or four strides, he'd caught up to her. "You actually saw someone?"

"I saw binoculars aimed at us. They were there when we arrived. Considering the kind of community this is, I would expect a neighbor to come down to check things out. And if it's a hiker, they should have moved on by now."

Was it possible that it was the killer?

Was that the reason the killer hadn't called 911 until this morning? Because he'd wanted to be able to catch the show?

Mark grabbed his cell phone and hit the speed dial for Larson. "There's someone up on the mountain showing a lot of interest. Might be our guy. Benedict and I are going up to check it out."

"Tell me where, and I'll—"

"No. Stay put. I need you to give him something to look at. Something to focus on down there so that he doesn't start looking elsewhere."

"Are you talking a diversion? Like what?"

"Drag the dead dog out in front of the house for starters. That will keep him busy for a few minutes."

"And after that?"

"Get creative if you have to. He sees us coming, he'll bolt."

Mark disconnected and reclipped the phone to his waist. He'd been letting Beth lead the way, but now increased his pace, overtaking her. "I go off course, you let me know."

He didn't like the whole setup. Being on the downgrade made them vulnerable, made them easy targets for anyone above them. He wasn't wearing a protective vest. Neither was she.

Which meant the only thing between them and a bullet might be Larson's diversion.

For more than five minutes they moved upward, negotiating the expected gauntlet of dense undergrowth and roots and logs. But then when they were a hundred yards into the trees, the trunks suddenly seemed to close ranks and the light that had previously penetrated the nearly nude branches overhead, leaked away, leaving them in damp shade. And from there, the going only got tougher, until they were limited to pushing forward single file.

Suddenly, still behind him, Beth veered to the right, planting her back hard against the trunk of the closest tree, motioning him to do the same.

Once he had, she pointed upward, indicating that she'd seen something or someone above them.

As Mark edged out, the material of his jacket scraped across the rough bark. At first, the only thing he could sort out was the lighter color of the bluff's rock face. It wasn't a huge outcropping, but enough that anyone on top would have a clear view of not only them, but also of the farmhouse below.

And then just when he became certain that there was nothing there, he saw a flash of red. A shirt maybe.

Ducking back behind the tree, he used hand signals to instruct Beth. He'd go in first. She'd hang back to provide cover.

Trying to limit his exposure, he advanced in a partial crouch. His first course of action was to get in as tight as possible to the rock formation. Once he had, whoever was up there would have to lean out far enough to also become exposed.

Once Mark reached the rock face, he glanced back, trying to determine Beth's position. As he watched, she scrambled almost silently to a location that would allow her a better angle in case she needed to lay down some cover fire.

His phone vibrated in his pocket. He ignored it.

Keeping his weapon pointed slightly upward, he stared at the ledge above as he continued to place one foot in front of the other.

From here on out, even with careful foot placement, there was no way his movements wouldn't be heard by whoever was up there. But large game was common in these woods, so there was always the chance he'd be mistaken for a deer or a bear crashing about in the underbrush.

Of course, some people shot those, too.

Chapter Eleven

Another burst of adrenaline hit Mark's system as leaves suddenly exploded over the edge, cascading down the rock face. The exodus was accompanied by scrambling footsteps overhead.

He'd obviously been spotted. And whoever was up there was either rushing to reach a more defensible position for a standoff or, even worse, attempting to escape.

Mark attacked the steep grade, the sound of his movements making it impossible to hear what was happening above him now.

Even as he climbed, he looked back once or twice, hoping to catch a glimpse of Beth somewhere behind him. But he couldn't.

Which didn't mean she wasn't there.

One moment he was dealing with the undergrowth and the next he was standing ankle-deep in loose rubble at the base of a thirty-foot rock wall. He could either swing left, hoping to find another more-passable route to the top, which would eat up time and might not result in a better option, or he could holster his weapon and, using two hands, start scaling.

If he could catch this guy, it could end right now. They could stop the killings.

He glanced over his shoulder. If Beth wasn't back there, wasn't in a position to cover him when he started climbing, he'd be shit out of luck.

Did he trust her with his life?

Did he believe what was in her personnel file, or did he trust his own assessment?

Deciding to go with what his gut told him, Mark tucked the automatic away, kicked out of his hard-soled shoes and, tying the shoelaces together, hung them around his neck.

Hurriedly scanning the wall, he searched for the best route, and then stretching for his first handhold nearly eight feet overhead, started the ascent.

Rock climbing required strength and skill and a certain amount of finesse even when using equipment, and without ropes and pitons, the sport quickly became more difficult and more deadly. It had been years since he'd attempted free climbing, but in most ways it was like riding a bike. Of course, if he fell off, the landing was going to be a hell of a lot harder.

Halfway up, his left foot suddenly slipped. The muscles of his fingers and hands and arms locked. With his face plastered to the rough stone, he fumbled, desperately trying to locate the foothold before his muscles gave out or the single foothold that was currently holding him up gave way.

When he finally recaptured the small edge of stone that was no more than an inch in depth, he shifted so that his weight was equally distributed over both feet. He slowly used his legs to push his body upward, reaching overhead for the next handhold, repeating the process over and over.

It wasn't until he got to within two feet of the ledge that

he stopped briefly to catch his breath. Glancing down and to the left, the only direction he could look given his current position, he scanned for Beth again, and then when he didn't see her, checked out the edge above. He listened intently for any sounds of movement, unable to quite shake the feeling that when he finally did reach the top, the only thing waiting would be a bullet.

But the odds of surviving a gunshot were probably better than those for a thirty-foot fall.

As he hoisted himself up and over, the first rifle crack rang out. Mark didn't see where the bullet struck the rock, but he felt the shards sting his right cheek. Two more shots rapidly followed.

And then, from somewhere below, came several answering rounds. Beth watching his butt, thank God. Mark dove toward the only cover he could reach, a log a dozen feet away. His shoes were ripped free.

Drawing his weapon, he listened in frustration as the shoes landed in the rubble below. In a standoff, being barefoot wouldn't matter. But in any type of pursuit, he damn sure was going to be screwed, and he could pretty well guarantee that's what they were looking at here. Otherwise, the shooter would have taken Mark out before he reached the ledge.

As far as the weapon the shooter was using, it had sounded like a twenty-two caliber rifle. A varmint weapon. Perhaps not the most deadly firearm out there, but at anything less than eighty yards, a well-placed shot could take down a man.

Had Beth actually seen the shooter, or had she just been firing blind, trying to make her presence known? Trying to give the shooter something to worry about?

Mark jerked the cell phone off his belt. As soon as he got a look at it, he realized he wasn't going to be reaching Beth or anyone else on it. At some point during the climb, he'd managed to trash it.

"Benedict?" Mark called.

No response.

Shit! Now what? Was she trying to find a way up?

Mark found himself wishing that it had been Larson and not Beth covering his back. Not because he didn't trust her to do her best, but because he wasn't completely sure how she'd handle the current situation.

Forced to consider his options, he stared up at the dirty gray clouds. The temperature was dropping. Or maybe it felt that way because his feet were bare, and he was stretched out on a cold slab of granite that suddenly seemed to offer all the comfort and warmth of a morgue table.

Doing a partial sit-up, he tried to see over the log while still maintaining a low profile. Another crack sounded. Mark dropped flat again as the bullet removed a chunk of log only inches from where his head had been seconds earlier.

A close miss by the shooter, or an intentional display of skill?

Either way, the round had come from the trees above him, from somewhere to the right of the wide strip of cleared land that was a utility easement.

He shifted sideways, enough that he could get a view of the top of the mountain, and quickly realized that he was screwed. That the shooter's position would make it possible for him to continue up the mountain while keeping Mark pinned down.

Mark grappled with his growing frustration.

Having heard the shots and now unable to reach Mark, Larson and the two agents down at the farmhouse would already be on their way up, possibly accompanied by Livengood and his deputies. But it would take them too long. At least ten minutes. With that kind of lead, the shooter could reach the summit. And the backdoor to an extensive forest.

So where in the hell was Beth? Where was his backup? He didn't like leaving her behind, but unless she showed in the next sixty seconds, that's exactly what he was going to be forced to do.

Hearing something scrabbling at the rock just below his position, he shifted sideways again so he could get a look over the edge. Though she sounded winded and was struggling, she was already within several feet of the top. As she settled into her current position on the wall, the shoes draped around her neck from the front thumped against her back. Not one pair, but two.

That he felt relieved to see her didn't surprise him. What did catch him off guard was the level of his relief.

As she looked up for her next handhold, she saw him and offered a tense smile.

"You're doing fine," he said.

"Yeah, well, I'm not so sure about that."

As she reached for the ledge, Mark quickly switched the SIG-Sauer to his weaker hand, leaving the stronger one free to grab the back of her jacket. "On the count of three you get your butt up here while I lay down some cover."

She gave no indication that she'd even heard him.

"One. Two." Mark lifted his weapon, squeezing off two rounds toward the trees while hauling her up next to him.

She collapsed in the dirt. Her chest continued to rise and fall rapidly as she tried to catch her breath. She'd shed her jacket before making the climb, so was down to a pink short-sleeved T-shirt.

As it had yesterday, her hair had begun to curl and the makeup she'd been wearing earlier was gone, revealing flushed, glowing skin. The bullet graze above her right temple was more pronounced, a visual reminder of what she'd faced during the past forty-eight hours. It was also an unpleasant reminder that he was solely responsible for making her this killer's target.

When she looked over at him, though, she was smiling and her eyes were bright.

He caught himself returning the smile. "Let me see your phone."

She passed it without comment. Mark punched in the only number he could recall off the top of his head. Larson answered on the second ring. "What in the hell's going on up there?"

"Right now? He's got us pinned down."

"Pinned down where?"

"You probably don't have a good visual of the bluff yet, but can you see the utility easement?"

"Yeah."

"He's on the right of it and headed to the top. In a few seconds we'll be going up the left-hand side." The cleared easement running up the mountain made a decent buffer and at the same time nearly eliminated the possibility of their walking into any type of ambush.

"Why don't you hang tight? We'll be there in five minutes, ten at the outside."

"Too long. He reaches the top, he's got a half-million acres to disappear into. Alert the park service. Have them shut down all roads. And get us some bloodhounds."

"Okay. Is Benedict there with you?"

"Yeah. She's fine."

As Mark ended the call and shoved the phone into his pocket, Beth passed him his shoes.

"Larson worried about me? Or is he concerned that I'm not taking good care of you?" she asked.

"He's a good agent."

"Didn't say he wasn't."

Mark worked at undoing the laces. "How are your legs holding up?"

"Better than my scraped-up feet." Rolling awkwardly onto her side, she shoved her shoes back on. "How do you want to do this?"

"We'll go together, but I'll take the lead. Try to stay behind me, okay?"

"I don't think he's looking to kill me. At least not yet. Where's the fun in that?"

He glanced over at her, surprised by just how loose she sounded. And just how comfortable he was having her as his backup. He motioned with his chin toward the top of the mountain. "There's a large pine leaning out into the utility easement. He's somewhere just below it."

Mark took off running, Beth only steps behind. A single sharp crack shattered the stillness.

Reaching the relative safety of the trees, Mark immediately set a grueling pace, this time unsurprised when she managed to stay with him.

Why only one shot when the shooter could have gotten off several more while they'd been out in the open?

Because the shooter felt his current lead was sufficient to guarantee his escape?

Or because he was low on ammo?

Or maybe killing them just wasn't on today's agenda.

Everything up until this morning had suggested an organized offender. The type of perp who carefully chose his targets in advance, spending weeks or maybe months researching them, planning for every contingency. And most important, always covering his tracks thoroughly.

So why had he allowed them to get so close this morning?

Mark scanned the opposite edge of the easement for their shooter.

"Do you see him?" Beth asked.

"No. He's probably moved back into the trees some, but it's unlikely he'll actually change his course." Grabbing a sapling, Mark used it to pull himself up the three-foot-high washout.

"So do you think this is how he came in? Through the forest?" Beth used the same small tree as a climbing aide. "That he has a vehicle waiting?"

"Even if he doesn't have one stashed somewhere in there, even if he hadn't planned to be spotted and now finds himself in need of an escape route, he might be planning to lose himself in there for a few days."

"He'd have to know the place will be crawling with law enforcement almost immediately."

"And he'd also know there's no way to completely secure five hundred thousand acres. If he's spent any time around here, which I suspect he has, chances are he'll know the area better than most of the manpower we bring in to find him. It wouldn't be all that difficult for him to slip by us."

Mark glanced up at the darkening sky. "Best chance we have of capturing him once he reaches the refuge is the dogs. That's assuming the weather holds off. If we get a good downpour, we might as well pack it in and wait for the next call, the next incident."

Not pushing quite so hard for a split second, he again searched for some movement in the trees above and to the right of them. This time he thought he saw something. Back in the shadows. And if he was right, the shooter had ditched the red shirt or jacket for one that was camo.

"Do you see anything?" Beth asked.

When Mark had slowed, she'd kept going and was now slightly above him. As she negotiated the loose soil and scrambled up the steeper grade, the muscles of her buttocks bunched and released rhythmically, the sight causing him to lose his concentration momentarily.

Because he wasn't a masochist, he lengthened his stride until he was shoulder to shoulder with her again. He'd always been an ass man. And even though he had no intention of acting on the attraction, there was no reason to pretend that it didn't exist. That he wasn't a man with a man's needs. Needs that hadn't been met in quite some time.

"He's still there," Mark said. "We may have gained some, but not enough."

"Must…must be in good shape."

He didn't comment on her observation. Mostly because he didn't want to waste the air in his lungs. He could do six miles on a treadmill with a twenty-degree incline, but the current grade was closer to fifty.

And the shooter was having no problem handling the steep and rough terrain while maintaining the pace. Which, at the very least, suggested that he was an outdoorsman. Someone comfortable in these mountains.

Was it someone who had shared Thesing's environmental concerns? Some extremist who hadn't shown up on the list they'd found in the chemist's home?

Beth nearly tripped on a root. Mark reached out to steady her, but she'd already caught herself.

She swiped at the sweat dripping in her eyes. "So do you think…it's possible…the reason he hung around… Because he wanted to see the body bags…hauled out? Proof of…of his success? Of…superiority?"

"Maybe." Mark's gut tightened as yet another thought entered his mind. One that now seemed to make complete sense to him.

Perhaps the reason the shooter had been on the bluff this morning had nothing to do with gloating or with watching body bags loaded into the backs of vehicles. Maybe the reason they'd managed to get so close was because the shooter didn't have time to plan things out quite as thoroughly as he normally did. Because up until 4 a.m. when he'd gotten off the phone with Beth, he hadn't intended to be anywhere near here this morning.

"Or maybe after calling you this morning—" He broke off long enough to drag in more air. "He wanted another look at you."

Out of the corner of his eye, he saw her lips tighten. Four months ago Rabbit Rheaume had tried to kill her. Two nights ago, he'd paid for a second attempt on her life. And now, only hours ago, she'd learned that she was again a marked woman.

No matter what the freak had said about letting her live, Mark didn't believe for a moment he would. Given the opportunity, this guy wouldn't hesitate to kill her. But in order to do it, he was damn well going to have to go through Mark.

Even as winded and leg weary as they were when they saw the first forest sign marking the western boundary of the Nantahala, they kept moving.

From here on out, things were only going to get more dicey. Gone was the easement's buffer of barren land that had made an ambush nearly impossible. Gone also was the dense underbrush that had provided at least some cover for them. All they had now were old-growth pines that towered above the ground.

He glanced down at the brown carpet of pine needles. With every square inch of ground covered by them, there weren't going to be any bootprints to point them in the right direction. And forget about hearing any sounds of movement this asshole might make.

Mark moved forward cautiously. Between the cloud cover and the tree cover, it looked like dusk, and if that wasn't bad enough, the tree trunks were big enough that a man could easily hide behind any one of them and step out at the last second.

As Beth started to spread out, moving away from him, he said, "We stay within ten feet of each other. No more."

She offered a silent nod.

Maybe he was just being paranoid, but he couldn't quite shake the feeling that instead of their chasing the shooter into the forest, they'd been skillfully led here by him.

How far behind were Larson and the rest of them at this point? From previous experience Mark knew that less time had passed than it felt like. Maybe only five or six minutes now. Time enough for Larson to reach the bluff, but not enough to get up the mountain.

There was a subtle sound to his right, like a twig cracking as it was stepped on. Mark motioned Beth to drop back some while he checked it out. As he got within five feet of the tree, a fox darted past him.

As Mark circled around the trunk, he first saw the rabbit's body at its base and then a few feet away the head that had been twisted off. Not by any fox, but by a man. His father had taken him hunting once or twice, so he'd seen the technique used, but he still found the sight slightly disturbing.

Backing away, he rejoined Beth.

"What did you find?"

"Dead rabbit."

"The fox?"

"No."

The scent of rain had been growing steadily stronger, but now so was the breeze. Pine needles floated down as the branches overhead swayed.

Mark glanced upward, briefly studying what he could see of the sky. "Weather doesn't look good."

Beth looked up quickly but didn't comment. But then she didn't have to. Because they both knew they were quickly running out of time. That rain was their enemy.

They managed to move carefully downslope for nearly a minute before it finally hit. But when it did, it was vicious. It pounded through the canopy, instantly soaking them as if buckets of water were being poured over them one after the other.

He wiped a hand down his face and then shoved the hair off his forehead. Talk about bad luck. "Whatever evidence there was, it's gone now. And after this, it's unlikely that even a bloodhound will be able to pick up anything."

Beth's mouth thinned. "We could continue in the direction we're headed for a few more minutes," she suggested. "We might get lucky."

He was beginning to believe that she didn't know how to stop. Though he'd always seen tenacity as a valuable trait for an agent to possess, personal experience had shown him that the reckless variety ended in either death or a commendation.

If he'd been alone, he might have been tempted to continue on, to put himself at risk, but he had no intention of putting her life on the line. Not when they were without protective vests and carried weapons that, while accurate and more powerful than a rifle at close range, became less so at greater distances.

And not when he suspected that they were being manipulated right into an ambush.

"To go after him we need to be better equipped. Warmer clothes, camouflage, body armor and assault weapons for starters."

When her mouth tightened, he knew she wasn't happy about the decision.

The cell phone in his pocket vibrated.

"Yeah."

It was Larson. "Unless you're on to something up there, you might want to come back and take a look at this."

"What is it?"

"I can tell you what it is. I just can't tell you what it means exactly."

Chapter Twelve

Larson met them at the bottom of the utility easement with their coats. "I thought you two might want these."

Beth didn't miss the look of speculation in Larson's gaze as he passed her jacket. Maybe he was beginning to recognize that he'd misjudged her.

"Thanks." Despite her soaked and muddy condition, she dragged it on. She was cold and tired and still frustrated by Mark's decision to break off the pursuit, but was determined to keep all those things to herself. She couldn't afford to reveal any sign of weakness. Nor did she plan to do anything that might seem to substantiate the lies in her personnel file.

"So what did you find?" Mark adjusted the collar on his suit coat.

"Come see." Larson headed for the bluff and the huge flat area of rock resembling a four-foot-high raised stage. Reaching it, he bound up easily, followed by Mark.

Once on top, Mark turned back, extending a hand down to her. They were both covered in mud and wet.

When she didn't reach up right away, he smiled. "I know it's not thirty vertical feet, but place your foot on that lip of rock, and I'll help you."

His fingers were strong and firm and not nearly as chilled as her own were. And as they closed around hers, a warmth flooded her veins. It wasn't as if they hadn't touched numerous times during the past half hour, but somehow it felt different this time. It felt more personal. More invasive.

He moved backward as he pulled her up, giving her room to land. But even when she was standing in front of him, with only inches separating them, he didn't let her go.

Perhaps because he thought she was too close to the edge and if he did, she'd lose her balance and slip backward. But the truth was she'd lost her balance around him three years ago. And even now when she was supposed to be this trained special agent, this professional law enforcement machine, he reminded her that beneath all that, she was still very much a woman.

"Thanks." When she made a move to step past him, he let go of her. In the next instant, though, she wished he hadn't. With the rock being so narrow, the movement had brought her uncomfortably close to the edge.

Even though she'd never particularly cared for extreme heights—especially the straight down and without railings variety like this one—they drew her in. Like a pretty picture compelling her to move closer.

She looked over and down onto the top of the trees below, her heart rate climbing again. Her gaze backtracked until it reached the miniaturized white clapboard farmhouse below. Lookouts didn't come any better than this one.

Turning, she got her first glimpse of what Larson had brought them to see—a lawn chair draped in a dark blanket. With a leaden sky as a backdrop and sitting on rock nearly the same shade of gray, the chair almost seemed to float in midair.

She managed to catch up to Mark before he reached Larson.

"I found the Ravenel name written on the chair and in the sleeping bag," Larson said.

Mark frowned. "See if we can determine from where on the property they were taken and if there's any way to narrow the time frame of when they were removed. I want to know if he's been sitting up here for days, watching, waiting for us to find the bodies? Or if he set this all up a few hours ago?"

Beth turned her face into the wind, using it to push the hair away from her cheeks. "Why would the timing matter?"

"Because, if the 911 call was his way of getting you out in the open, it suggests that he's becoming fixated on you. It explains his sloppiness this morning."

"And what if he is obsessed with me?"

"Then we'll use it to our advantage. See if we can force him into being sloppy again."

Fixated. Obsessed. She'd never considered those words particularly scary, but in the present context they certainly carried some menacing undertones.

She didn't bother to ask why she'd been singled out. The only person who could answer that question with any authority was their unsub. And maybe he didn't fully understand the reasons behind his own behavior. Obsessions rarely had any foundation in reality, were instead based on skewed perceptions.

Squatting next to the chair, Mark reached under, nudging a section of orange peel out into the open. "Seems our guy likes fresh fruit."

Beth dropped down next to him. "Looks like there's enough here for more than one orange."

Now Larson joined them, peering under the chair. "There was a bowl of them on Ravenel's kitchen table."

"See if they're the same kind. And find out if the Ravenels had a .22 caliber rifle."

She shifted her gaze toward the farm nearly a thousand feet below.

Is that what the shooter had been doing as he watched the bodies of his victims carted out? Had he sat here calmly peeling and eating stolen oranges? Treating what was happening below as entertainment?

Her chest tightened at the idea. Somehow she knew she was right, though. And for the first time she acknowledged her apprehension. The phone call last night had initially unsettled her, but by this morning she'd felt mostly empowered by it. Because it seemed to guarantee that she'd get what she'd been wanting most. The opportunity to prove herself.

But at what cost?

Because it was bound to be less unsettling than her current thoughts, she forced herself to refocus on what Mark and Larson were discussing.

"There'll be fifty agents here in the next hour and an additional thirty by nightfall," Larson said. "The forest service has been alerted and all roads in or out of the area are being closely monitored. But I've got to tell you, Gerritsen, even with all that... These are the same mountains that Abe Rutherford disappeared into after bombing those three clinics six years ago. There were two hundred agents swarming all over the Nantahala Forest for months with no results."

Mark straightened. "This guy isn't Rutherford. He's not looking to disappear. He's looking to make a name for himself. I just want to make sure he doesn't do it by piling up bodies."

ELEVEN HOURS LATER, the sun having sunk hours ago behind the towering pines and the mountains, Mark and Beth, along with a large task force of both local and federal law enforcement officers walked out of the Nantahala Forest cold, tired and hungry.

And with nothing to show for their efforts.

With eighty-two additional FBI agents having joined the investigation in the past eight hours, there weren't enough hotel rooms in Bellingham. So many of them would be driving treacherous mountain roads for nearly an hour to find a bed. And at daybreak they'd be back. A pattern that would continue until either the killer was captured, or there was definitive proof that he was no longer hiding in the forest.

The most likely *proof* of his defection would come with an extremely high price tag—more victims.

Beth left Mark talking to a forest ranger at the picnic pavilion. With the vehicles in the parking lot rapidly thinning out, the restrooms would be locked up shortly.

She passed a couple of local deputies and several FBI agents on the trail, but there were fewer of them than earlier.

As she walked into the ladies' room, Special Agent Jenny Springer was standing at the closest sink. Like the rest of them, she was dressed in jeans, boots and a black baseball cap with FBI across the front of it.

Glancing over as the door dropped closed behind Beth, Jenny shook the water off her hands. "This is the first time in years I've been involved in the actual manhunt, and today was my wake-up call. I need to get back in the gym on a regular basis." She grabbed a handful of toilet paper to dry her hands on. "But I heard you scored one for our gender."

At Beth's perplexed expression, Jenny said, "Thirty-foot free climb and keeping up with Mark Gerritsen. Not many women can do that." She removed her cap, ran a hand across the top of her head as if trying to fluff her flattened hair. "Must have been unsettling. Getting that call last night. Talking to our guy."

"Sure." Beth started to fold her arms in front of her, but then didn't, aware that Jenny would recognize the body language. Would know that the current topic made her anxious.

"But you're having second thoughts about it now? Wondering if you're up to the challenge?"

Beth didn't say anything for several seconds, slightly shaken by Jenny's analysis. Mostly because it was dead-on. For most of the afternoon, she'd been thinking about the next phone call, trying to prepare herself emotionally for it. And had been worried that when the time came, she'd fail. And because she did, more people would die.

She would die.

Jenny studied her briefly. "You're wondering if you have what it takes?"

"I suppose I am."

"I'm just going to be blunt here. I've heard some of the rumors that have been circulating about your recent troubles with Monroe. That kind of thing can really undercut an agent's confidence. Make her question every move she makes. Every decision. And when cases are discussed, she starts holding back, afraid if she opens her mouth, she'll look incompetent." Jenny paused. "I haven't seen anything to suggest there's any truth to those rumors."

She pulled the hat back on. "I've worked with Gerritsen a number of times. He's no fool. If he didn't think you could handle it, you wouldn't be here."

Jenny opened the outside door. "Want me to wait for you?"

Beth shook her head. "No. I'll be fine. I'll be right behind you."

Several minutes later Beth removed the baseball cap, leaving it on the edge of the sink while she splashed water on her face. Jenny's vote of confidence had taken her by surprise and, more important, made her reexamine her actions over the past four months. Beth realized she'd been holding back. She'd been analyzing and questioning herself endlessly. Monroe had taken lies and nearly made them truths. But only because she'd let him.

Since her arrival in Bellingham, though, she'd begun to trust herself again.

Tossing the wad of tissue she'd used to wipe her face into the trash, she stepped back outside. Perhaps it was only that she'd just left a lighted space, but the trail seemed darker.

Unzipping her jacket to make her weapon more accessible, she hesitated, making excuses for her sudden and unwarranted jumpiness. She was tired. Kind words had lowered her defenses. A faceless monster planned to kill her. Only the last of those could actually harm her, and she didn't for a minute believe the monster was anywhere near by.

He was too smart for that.

Almost as soon as Beth stepped from beneath the overhang and headed toward the pavilion, the night went from dark to bathed in soft light. Glancing up, she realized a full moon had just breached the mountain to the east and seemed to teeter atop the saw tooth silhouettes of towering pines.

The sight made her slow and then come to a complete stop.

In the relative stillness, she could hear the Nantahala Falls crashing through the gorge a mile away. Nantahala. The Cherokee word for *land of the noon-day sun*. She'd been in North Carolina for a day and a half now, but the vastness of the forest, the deep, deep gorges that saw only fleeting sunlight when the sun was straight overhead, had completely awed her. And now this moon.

She couldn't recall the last time she'd seen one quite so huge.

The hairs at the back of her neck came to attention, but it happened so slowly that she thought a breeze was responsible. Until she heard the first real rustle that couldn't be attributed to the wind.

She searched the deeper shadows beneath the trees in front of her. Her heart slammed hard behind her ribs, its rate climbing even as she tried to rein it in. Even as she told herself that it was just a foraging animal. A raccoon looking to check out the trash cans.

Slipping her hand inside her jacket, she reached for her gun just as a man's shape separated itself from the trees. Her chest tightened, but not nearly as hard as her fingers did on her weapon. She left it holstered, waiting for some sign of his intentions.

He took an additional step toward her. "Sorry. I didn't mean to frighten you."

"You didn't," she lied. The only thing she could really make out was his rangy build. Who was he? What was he doing out here?

He motioned up. "It's an exquisite sight, isn't it? Some in these parts call it a hunter's moon."

As he walked toward her, she left her hand resting on her weapon. Because he never completely moved out from beneath the trees, even when he got to within seven or eight feet of her, she still couldn't see his face clearly. But she recognized his forest ranger jacket. She'd probably met him at some point during the day, but there was nothing particularly familiar about him.

Exhaling, she let go of her weapon and forced her lips into a welcoming smile. "Come to lock up the restrooms?" she asked, still unable to completely shake her nervousness.

"Yes. And your boss asked me to check on you. To see if you were okay."

For the first time in several minutes, she was able to take a deep breath. She had nothing to be uneasy about. Mark had sent the ranger.

"I'm okay." She almost felt foolish now. "Thanks. I was just heading back." She rezipped her coat and shoved her bare hands into the deep pockets.

"Good night, then," he offered as he started toward the restrooms.

"I've heard of a harvest moon and a blue one, but why a hunter's moon?"

He turned back at the question. "They call it that because it's so big and bright that even nocturnal animals become easy prey."

"Makes sense, I guess." She walked backward a step or two. "Well. Have a good night."

"You, too."

She was nearly to the pavilion when she remembered leaving her hat in the restroom and went back to get it.

Chapter Thirteen

"So this sector is the least accessible region of the forest?" Mark asked, pointing to an area dead center of the large map. Lifting his gaze, he waited for the ranger on the opposite side of the picnic table to respond.

Because of the breeze and the poor lighting under the pavilion, two battery lanterns not only provided the needed light but also held down the edges of the map.

A propane heater had been brought in earlier to warm the space—an impossible task, given that it was an open structure. Several minutes ago, though, it had run out of fuel.

Straightening, the ranger folded his arms across his chest and tucked his hands into his armpits. "That's certainly the worst terrain, but there are others that are darn near as bad."

"But if our guy is familiar with the Nantahala and is looking to dig in for a few weeks, is this where he's likely to head?"

"Abe Rutherford was out there for sixteen months. But we're talking someone who was an army ranger and had survival skills."

"I think it's a fairly safe bet our guy has similar training."

Mark already had several agents working that angle,

pulling records of anyone from the area who had been in the armed services, focusing especially on those dishonorably discharged.

The ranger offered a tight nod. "Rutherford had two safe houses set up before he ever bombed the first clinic. If he hadn't, there's no way he could have survived a winter out there."

Was that what their guy had been doing the past few months? Establishing a base camp to operate out of? A place to return to after each strike? If that was the case, he would have begun stockpiling supplies sometime after early July. In a large city, a change of buying habits would go unnoticed, but here in Bellingham, they might not.

The ranger motioned toward the large thermos of coffee sitting on a nearby table. "I'm going to grab some. Can I bring you another cup?"

Mark shook his head. "It's late and I'm sure you're beat. For now, I think you've answered most of my questions."

"If you have more, I'll be here in the morning."

As the ranger walked off, Mark glanced at the map once more, focusing on the red dot marking the Ravenel home. If the killer was local, why start in Bellingham? Why not leave those targets closest to his base until last? He'd have to know that once he revealed himself, the manhunt would be unrelenting.

But then, nothing about this guy really seemed to add up. He wasn't acting like an extremist. His only targets so far appeared to be personal ones. He possessed a weapon capable of killing thousands at a time, but killed only a few, even if he'd aimed to kill the whole boys' basketball team, that was only twelve people. And now he wanted to make a game out of it.

Mark rubbed his lower face. It was like trying to build a house of cards from the top down. Unless you were a magician, it couldn't be done.

Maybe what he needed to do was give it a rest for an hour. Think about something else. Checking his watch, he discovered it was after nine already.

He still hadn't heard back from his attorney. Should he try phoning Traci? If she'd cooled down some, maybe he could convince her to work things out without getting any lawyers involved. She'd come around in the past, perhaps this time wouldn't be any different.

It was too late now, though. He'd have better luck calling in the morning when Addison and Gracie were busy with their video games. An unexpected and raw sense of nostalgia rolled over him as he thought about long-ago winter mornings when they'd watched cartoons in the family room while he fixed their breakfast. The way they'd giggled at the bunny-shaped pancakes. The way the scent of syrup had lingered in the kitchen for most of the day.

He loved his daughters more than anything in the world. But the truth was, he'd let them down. He'd been putting his job before them. Not for just the past four months, but for nearly a year now. Pretending that making the world a better place, a safer place, was more important than being there for them.

He obviously needed to make some changes in his life.

Lifting a lantern, he released one edge of the map, letting it roll up on its own.

It was time to pack it in, to head back to the hotel with Beth and wait for a phone call.

He glanced toward the picnic table where she'd headed after she'd grabbed the last cup of coffee. A group of searchers had come back late, and she'd gone over to talk to them. Not seeing her there, he shifted his gaze to the people near the walkway, his heart rate still normal but already beginning to climb.

Even with the poor lighting, as they parted and headed for the cars, he knew she wasn't among them.

The fatigue he'd been feeling seconds earlier vanished.

Where the hell was she? She wasn't to leave the pavilion for any reason without checking with him. He'd been very clear about it.

Hearing footsteps behind him, he turned. She'd just entered the pavilion and strolled toward him in that somewhat aggressive stride of hers. Even if he hadn't been able to see her face, he would have known her just by the way she moved. She stopped by the picnic table where the last three searchers had climbed to their feet, preparing to leave.

Trying to restrain his temper, Mark rolled up the map the rest of the way. By the time she reached him, he'd tamped down some of his anger, but not all of it.

"Looking for me?" she asked.

"You weren't to leave this pavilion without me. When I give an order, I expect it to be followed." He wrapped the rubber band around the map. "Without question." He nailed her with his gaze. "You understand?"

She didn't say anything for several seconds. He'd obviously blindsided her. He didn't know why, though. She should have known he'd be upset when she ignored a command.

"I went to the bathroom, not wandering out into the woods." Her mouth flattened. "I'm in no more danger now than I was in the parking garage two nights ago. I handled that situation. And I'll handle the next one."

"You damned well weren't my responsibility then."

The words hung between them for several seconds, long enough for Mark to realize just how loudly he'd said them. And that he was thankful that it was only the two of them in the pavilion now.

Beth ducked her head, running her hand through her hair. Meeting his gaze, she spoke in a tone that may not have been calm, but was certainly controlled. "And your only responsibility now is as my senior officer."

Faced with her composure, Mark managed to get a foothold into his own. "We both know my culpability goes beyond that. That I hold at least partial blame. If I hadn't shoved you out there in front of him, he wouldn't even know you exist."

"And if he didn't, where would this investigation be?" She folded her arms. "Let's get one thing straight here. You may have requested the transfer, but I consider it an opportunity. One that I was lucky to get."

Frowning, he stepped in closer. "The chance to be bait?"

"No." Her gray eyes narrowed slightly as she lifted her chin to meet his gaze. "The chance to do my job. The opportunity to pursue a career that I happen to love."

He scanned her face. How in the hell could he argue with any of it? Hadn't she proven herself more than once today?

Hell. Maybe he was overreacting here. She was a trained FBI agent. One who hadn't hesitated to use lethal force when it was necessary. And he really had no reason to believe the man they hunted would come after her. Not this early in the game.

But when he'd looked up and been unable to find her...

He glanced away, troubled by the direction of his thoughts. But when he looked back, she was running a hand through her hair again, briefly exposing her right temple and the bullet graze just above it.

His gut tightened. She didn't seem to recognize just how damn close she'd come two nights ago.

He reached out, resting his fingers against her cheek. She seemed startled by the contact, her eyes first widening as they met his and then almost immediately narrowing, becoming guarded again.

Her skin was unbelievably soft beneath his fingertips and cool. He'd wanted to touch her a dozen times in the past forty-eight hours, but something had always stopped him—maybe only the desire to do the right thing.

So what in the hell was he doing now?

"I know you believe the reason it was Leon Tyber dead on that garage floor and not you was all the drills you ran in Hogan's Alley and the hours you spent on the shooting range."

He brushed his thumb along her right cheekbone, just missing the injury. "But the truth is…you came within an inch of losing your life. It could just as easily have been you on that floor."

His chest tightened as he imagined what it would have been like to find her body sprawled on the cold concrete instead of Tyber's.

She angled her chin up a bit more. Since it was her usual MO, he assumed it was with the intention of refuting his words, but she didn't. Instead she stood there mutely. He liked her chin, the way it popped up when she was challenged, like a fighter daring you to take your best shot. And even sexier, the soft, feminine cleft at its end.

When her bare lips softened and then parted, he realized the tightness in his chest no longer had anything to do with anger or concern.

He shifted his gaze to where he was touching her. He shouldn't be. Not like this. Nor should he be thinking about sleeping with her, but God help him, he was. And there was nothing abstract about it. He was imagining her firm thighs locked around him. Her tight abdomen rising up to meet him. Her harsh breathing in his ear as she came beneath him.

And from what he saw in her dark eyes, she was, too.

As if she'd been holding her breath, she suddenly exhaled, the warmth of it brushing the underside of his wrist. The sensation climbed his arm and shot deep into his body where the fantasies of seconds earlier already had him half-hard.

Unable to stop himself, he brushed his thumb over her bare lips and then slowly dipped his mouth toward hers. As their lips met, hers softened beneath his. She tasted like coffee.

Reaching out, his hand closed over her right hip, his fingertips flexing against denim as he tugged her nearer, deepening the kiss.

Wrapping her arms around his neck, she shifted in even closer, her breathing as ragged as his own. Her mouth opened beneath his as her abdomen brushed against his arousal. He felt control skating beyond his grasp. She was so damned sexy.

Pulling back, he looked into her eyes. They were as dark and as desperate as his own. Sliding his fingers through her hair, he lowered his lips to hers again and kissed her deeply, fiercely.

Her cell phone went off, the ring tone surprisingly loud. He felt her flinch with the second ring, and before it rang a third time, she was pulling away. He didn't hesitate to let her go.

And by the time it rang a fourth time, his regret had already set in. Backing away, she answered it.

"Yes, Father." Turning, she took several more steps, casting an uncomfortable glance over her shoulder as she moved away. "I got the message and I was planning to call."

She rubbed her forehead. "When?" Her voice dropped, the strain coming through for the first time. "Later, I guess. When I got back to the hotel."

As she listened, she paced several more feet, and because she still had her back to him, he watched her.

"Is that what Monroe told you? That the reassignment was temporary?"

Mark grabbed the map, wondering about not only the relationship between Beth and her father, but the one between her father and Bill Monroe, too. Why was Bill Monroe talking to Beth's father about things he clearly had no right to?

"Are you suggesting that you've been in contact with my doctor? That would be a clear violation of HIPPA."

Her shoulders stiffened. "But I didn't ask you to call their office, did I?"

She went silent for several seconds, and then said in an angry tone, "This conversation is over."

Even after she ended the call, she didn't face him right away, and he assumed that she was trying to collect herself.

Something inside him wanted to reach out to her, but he held it in check. He'd known that touching her would be a mistake and that kissing her would be an even bigger one.

Because now that he had, there was no way to go back, to pretend it hadn't happened.

Or to pretend that he didn't want it to happen again.

MARK HELD OPEN the door to the pizza joint. After the long day outside, when Beth stepped into the unexpected warmth, the aromas were welcoming. She scanned the interior. Quite a few tables were covered in the remnants of recent meals, but there were no other actual diners. Country music played on what sounded like a cheap radio in the kitchen. The sign outside had said they closed at ten and it was already nine-forty.

Before they'd entered the restaurant, she hadn't been all that hungry, but now her stomach growled.

A waitress stuck her head out the kitchen door. "Seat yourselves."

Mark motioned toward a back corner booth. "Why don't we try that one?"

Beth offered a silent nod and headed for it, aware of him just behind her as she wound her way through the tables in the center of the room. She dug her hands a little deeper into her pockets as she walked.

He'd spent most of the drive back to town on his cell phone, checking in with agents who hadn't been involved in the manhunt today, who'd been given other assignments instead. And she'd been extremely thankful that he'd been otherwise engaged because it had given her some time to pull herself together.

She'd known from the beginning that she was attracted to him and known that it wasn't completely one sided. And that getting involved with him on anything but a professional level would be stupid.

If you want something badly enough, you'll go against your best judgment.

Which is exactly what she'd done. And what she couldn't let happen again.

From the vibes he was giving off and the way he so carefully avoided any type of physical contact with her, she assumed he regretted the kiss every bit as much as she did.

Regretting and forgetting were two entirely different things, though.

Before sliding into the booth, she peeled off the heavy coat. The waitress had trailed behind and after explaining that the oven would be shut down soon, took their order.

Beth waited for the mugs of beer to be delivered before asking, "Has anything turned up yet connecting Thesing to the Ravenels?"

"No." He took a long sip. "And the list of ex-military with connections to this area is a long one. It will probably take twenty-four hours to check out everyone on it."

"What about you? Did you do any time in the military?"

"I did four years before going to college. Even after we moved away from the farm, money was always tight."

He rubbed his jaw, the action drawing attention to the five-o'clock shadow, reminding her how the slight stubble had felt against her skin.

"How'd you end up in counterterrorism?"

"I was three blocks from ground zero when 9/11 happened. I requested a transfer the next morning."

Having finished his beer, he relaxed back and folded his hands on the table between them. "What is the relationship between your father and Bill Monroe?"

The question caught her so completely off guard that the bottom of the mug clacked against the table top as she set it down. She knew he was scrutinizing her, so avoided looking up.

She debated not responding, but in all fairness, he had put a lot on the line when he'd requested her transfer, so maybe she owed him an answer.

Inhaling sharply, she fought the growing tightness in her lungs, worried that when she'd finished with this question, he'd ask her about the reason behind Bill Monroe's vendetta.

"There is no relationship between my father and Monroe beyond the occasional phone call," she answered cautiously. "And I need to start by explaining that my mother wasn't American and had grown up in a society where women deferred without question to their men." Her mouth tightened, recalling her mother's courage when it came to her daughter, to seeing that Beth was raised differently. "She was the kind of wife my father wanted. She was never a true partner, but more a facilitator. She made his life easy. Was a beautiful and consummate hostess. All of which were desirable qualities in a diplomat's wife."

She took a sip of beer. "Some people think it was my father's decision that I be raised in the States, spending only summers overseas with them."

Mark leaned forward. "But it wasn't?"

"No. It was my mother." She inhaled softly. "She sent me to live with my father's parents, allowed them to raise her daughter because she wanted me to be completely American. She always used to say that freedom wasn't just a state of being it was a state of mind. Even when he retired and they were living full-time in the States, she never could make that transition. In her mind she always had to defer to him."

She looked away. Had she really needed to tell him all that? To go into quite that much detail?

"When I was released from the hospital four months ago, I spent fourteen days pretending I was okay and fourteen nights waiting for Rabbit Rheaume to send someone to kill me. I decided to take vacation time, go home for a few weeks. The security at my father's place is the best money can buy. I was hoping a different environment and a feeling of safety might help me turn the corner. And I guess because I'd only seen him twice during the time I was working the Rheaume case, I was hoping to spend some time with my father. To reconnect. We had several long talks, in some of them I revealed too much. He ordered me to resign from the FBI. When I refused, he went behind my back and called Bill Monroe."

"And said what?"

"That I was having nightmares. That I'd told him that I was concerned about my ability to function. It wasn't that my father lied, it was just the idea that when my back was against the wall, he turned his on me, too." She nudged the mug to one side. "We'll get beyond it eventually."

Even as she said those words, she realized just how foolish they were. Tomorrow was guaranteed to no one.

Her least of all.

IT WAS AFTER 3:00 a.m. when Beth scrambled out of bed, dragging half the covers onto the floor in the process.

For the past hour she'd been staring at the black void overhead, unable to shake the feeling the ceiling was slowly pressing down on her like a junkyard crusher. And that the reason she couldn't breathe was because the room had become so small it no longer held enough oxygen.

Logically she knew the ceiling hadn't moved and that there was plenty of air, but somehow all the logic in the world wasn't enough right now. She needed fresh air.

With desperate, unsteady hands, she jerked an oversize sweatshirt over her T-shirt and running shorts. She couldn't seem to get warm. It was as if there was this big block of ice somewhere deep inside her that just kept radiating cold.

Why in the hell did she have to have a panic attack tonight? With Mark in the adjoining room? With only an unlocked door between them?

Trying to hold on to the last edges of her self-control, she pulled on the sliding glass door, letting it creep soundlessly along the metal track. She couldn't let him see her. Not like this. She knew what she looked like right now. Frantic. Out of control.

Even when she had the door open, she didn't step outside. Instead, she sagged just inside. The first frigid blast of air on her bare legs was brutal, but the first cauterizing lungful was pure heaven. And after several minutes, the raw panic began to fade. Enough that she finally could concentrate on the landscape. It was a serene scene, the rolling lawn stretching uphill until it reached a line of hemlocks above. The light frost on the grass looked silvery in the moonlight.

She breathed deeply and evenly. Nights were always the worst. Without the distractions of duties to be fulfilled, of immediate challenges to be met, there was too much time to think. And worse still, to remember the terror of being locked inside a car trunk, the odor of burning leather seats, of animal skin, reaching her…knowing that she would be next.

But tonight her subconscious had served up new images, those of the two plumbers and of the Ravenels. Maybe it was because she'd come so close to dying that she could almost physically feel the emotional anguish and terror of their last moments on earth.

And now she was waiting for a call from the man who had so callously orchestrated those deaths. He'd said he might spare her, but she knew better.

Only one of them would survive.

Why her, though? Why had he chosen her?

Her chest had already started to tighten again when the door between the two adjoining rooms slowly opened. Glancing over, she saw Mark's silhouette. When he'd heard her moving around, had he assumed she'd received another call from the killer?

"Can't sleep?" he asked quietly.

"No." Turning to face him, she was surprised to see that he wore sweat bottoms that rode low at his lean hips and nothing else. The milky-blue light of the moon coming through the glass revealed every well-defined muscle of his chest and abdomen. She hurriedly glanced away, snugging her arms in front of her. Any other time, just looking at him might have made it possible to at least briefly push more lethal thoughts to the side, but not tonight.

"Want company?"

"Sure." She would have preferred to turn down the offer. To roll up into herself to hide. But she suspected refusing would only make him curious.

Stepping past her, he leaned against the wall on the opposite side of the slider, facing her. She glanced at him quickly, but then turned her attention back outside again, pretending there was something out there that intrigued her.

After several seconds he leaned toward her, the action probably meant to capture her attention. "You know there's a possibility that he won't call tonight, that we've thrown him off his game. At least temporarily."

"I know," she said, still staring outside. "Rutherford went to ground for sixteen months before he was captured. Hid out in these mountains. Survived on salamanders and acorns. I hope this time is different."

Out of the corner of her eye, she saw him frown. "Sixteen months without a bombing? Without innocent people losing their lives? I'll take that any day."

She knew he was right.

But if this killer disappeared for months and months, or even years…She forced air a little deeper into her lungs. She'd given nearly two years of her life to the Rheaume investigation, dealing with the stress and the knowledge that if her cover was blown Rabbit would kill her. She didn't want to spend a similar amount of time waiting for this killer to resurface, always looking over her shoulder, wondering if he was right behind her, wondering if in the next instant she was going to wind up like his other victims.

She'd been isolated for so long, first because of an investigation that made it a necessity and then because of the fallout from that same investigation. For the past four months, previous friends had been reaching out to her, but she'd turned them away. Afraid for their safety. Afraid that if Rheaume tried again, someone she cared about might get hurt.

What if she hadn't been alone in that garage two nights ago?

She didn't even realize there were tears on her cheeks until he was pulling her into his arms, against his lean body. Despite the way he radiated the warmth, the strength she so desperately needed, her arms remained limp at her sides. After months and years of relying on only her own stores of strength, she didn't know how to accept it from him.

"Shush," he said, his voice pitched low and slightly rough. "It's going to be okay."

She tried to smother the first harsh sob against his chest, tried to push the next one back down her throat, but it was no good. Now that one of them had escaped, there was no stopping the rest. Her hands crept up to his waist, rested there for several seconds with curled fingers before she finally wrapped her arms around him and held on tight.

She didn't try to lie to herself. The tears weren't for other people. They were selfish ones. She was just so damned tired of it all. Of fighting for her job, her life.

"Shush. Nothing's going to happen to you. I won't let it."

She wanted to believe him. Wanted to be able to trust that somehow he could protect her. But the truth was, even he wasn't safe.

Especially when he stood between her and the man they hunted.

His arms stayed locked around her until her sobs faded. Until her muscles loosened. Until she became aware that his hands ran slowly up and down her back.

Embarrassed, she attempted to back away. "I'm sorry. I don't…"

"There's nothing for you to be sorry about." Opening his arms, he still didn't let her go, his right hand closing on her left shoulder.

"Come on." He turned her toward the bed. "Let's get you warm."

Chapter Fourteen

After tucking her in, pulling the sheet and blanket up around her chin, Mark crossed to the sliding glass door, intending to close the curtains.

"Please don't," she said.

"Okay." He turned toward the door connecting their rooms.

"I meant please don't leave. I want you to stay."

He glanced over his shoulder, his gaze connecting with hers. The moonlight coming through the slider didn't quite reach the bed, so he couldn't really see her face. But then, he didn't have to. Everything he needed to know had been in her voice. She didn't want to be alone. She was still dealing with demons. And after the kiss earlier, he was dealing with a few of his own.

As he approached the bed, she shifted, making room. But as soon as she had, she lay back and closed her eyes.

It was only then that he realized what asking him had probably cost her.

Stretching out next to her, he pulled the covers over them both.

She was scared. He understood that. Anyone in her situation would be frightened. What he didn't fully understand was why she believed she shouldn't be afraid. Why she thought that justified fear made her weak.

"Talk to me," she said in the silence. "About anything."

It sounded like such a simple request, but it wasn't. Plenty of things came to mind. Like how he'd been awake for hours before he'd heard her get out of bed. Only, it hadn't been the anticipation of a killer's phone call robbing him of sleep. It had been the knowledge that she was only steps away. That there wasn't even a locked door between them. And that after the kiss earlier, odds were she wouldn't refuse him.

Even though her invitation had nothing to do with sex, his body had still gone hard. God. He should never have kissed her. Because now that he had, he couldn't get her out of his mind. Couldn't stop thinking about not just how sexy she was, but also how competent and resilient and…interesting. He'd noticed that trait when she'd been his student.

She stirred beside him, the mattress bouncing lightly as she turned to face him. "Tell me about your daughters."

"What do you want to know?"

"Do you get to see them much?"

"No. Not as much as I should. It's been seven weeks this time." And he didn't know how many more would go by before he'd get back to Virginia. So much depended on what happened with the investigation.

"Is that what your ex-wife was upset about? Your not seeing them enough?"

He'd known Beth had overheard part of the phone call, so her question didn't surprise him. What did was that he was telling her any of this.

"I was supposed to have the girls this weekend, should

have picked them up today after school. It was the third time that I canceled like that. Traci was worried how the girls were going to take it." He looked over at Beth. "When I wasn't able to make it the last time, Gracie became convinced that something had happened to me. That I wasn't ever coming home again." He ran a hand roughly over his face. "Traci had to deal with the fallout. It's hard on her." He paused.

"It's obviously hard on you, too," Beth said.

Mark reached out, brushing his fingers along Beth's cheekbone. "You and me, we see some pretty tough things. But I've discovered one of the hardest of all is seeing my daughter scared. Seeing anyone you care about scared is hard," he corrected. "Especially when they believe it means they're less than they should be."

His thumb brushed across her lips. "You're a very courageous woman, Beth. Don't let anyone convince you otherwise."

She started to turn away, but he wouldn't let her. "Being brave doesn't mean being without fear and never asking for help. We all have to sometimes." He smoothed her hair away from her face. "Why did Monroe assign you to the Rheaume case? You were less than thirteen months out of the academy."

She stiffened immediately. "You should ask him," she answered evasively.

"I'm asking you to trust me."

She rolled onto her back again and seemed to stare at the ceiling for more than a minute. "You remember that harbor bombing two years ago?"

"Sure."

"While working another case, I received a tip about a possible problem. I presented it to Bill Monroe. He said I wasn't to follow up on it, that he'd assign the lead to someone else. Someone with more experience. But he didn't. And I didn't find out until it was too late." She paused, this time glancing over at him. "I confronted him. He denied everything. And when I tried to take it to his boss, he made sure I couldn't. Made sure that it looked as if I had never given him the information in the first place. That I was the one who'd screwed up."

Mark had never liked the prick. "So he sent you undercover?"

She had looked away, but now glanced over at him again. "Yeah. I think he was hoping that Rabbit Rheaume would make me go away."

The anger that had been slowly building exploded inside him. Before he was through with Monroe, the man would wish he'd never met Beth.

Mark rolled onto his side and pulled her close. "I think it's time we both tried to get some sleep."

When the alarm on his phone went off in the next room hours later, he'd been awake for several minutes, but Beth was still sleeping peacefully. He couldn't recall the last time he'd shared a bed with a woman when it hadn't included sex. But then, what they'd managed to share fully dressed was more intimate than any sex act.

Beth stirred slightly as the alarm fell silent. It would go off again in five minutes. He'd let her sleep a few minutes more.

What was it about her that made him want to share parts of himself that he normally didn't?

When he and Traci had been first married, he'd brought aspects of his job home. He'd needed someone to talk to and she was the obvious choice. But he'd soon discovered his mistake. All the sharing may have been helping him, but not Traci. He'd wake up in the middle of the night and find her silently crying, worried that something would happen to him. That one night he wouldn't come home. It was easy to draw the parallel with what Gracie was going through right now.

Within months of entering the FBI, he stopped talking about his work and began to pretend that the investigations he'd been assigned were easier and safer. He and Traci had settled into a routine that in the end was at least partially responsible for their marriage falling apart.

Still mostly asleep, Beth groaned softly. She was flat on her stomach, her face half-buried in her pillow. As she opened her eyes, blinking even though the room was still mostly shadows, she met his gaze and smiled sleepily. "I can't believe I slept." She pushed up on her elbows. "What time is it?"

"About six-thirty." He traced the crease that sleep had left on her cheek. "You're beautiful in the morning, you know that?" Her eyes went dark as he leaned over and covered her mouth with his own. He had meant to give her just a quick wake-up kiss—all they had time for. But as soon as his lips brushed hers, her mouth opened under his, wet and welcoming. Jesus. She was sexy. Especially as she was now. Warm. Still muzzy with sleep. Not as guarded as she was when wide awake.

But unfortunately he was wide-awake. He knew that he was playing with fire. And that he wouldn't be the one who ended up burned. He couldn't do that to her. She had enough to contend with. She needed the other members of the unit to see her as the capable agent that she was, not as the woman in his bed.

She'd been hurt enough by jerks like Monroe. And even by her father. Mark had no intention of being the next in line.

It took everything inside him to pull back, to roll away from her soft body. From the raging need in his own.

When he glanced over his shoulder, she was already sitting on the opposite edge of the bed, her stiffly held back to him. He left without saying a word, pulling the connecting door closed as he went.

BETH JERKED THE BRUSH through her damp hair. She usually spent more than fifteen minutes drying it, torturing it smooth, but this morning she didn't have the patience for it. And the baseball cap would destroy her efforts, anyway.

When she'd gone back for her hat last night, she'd found the restroom door still unlocked but the cap gone. And no sign of the ranger.

She grabbed a spare cap. Gathering her hair in a rough ponytail, she slipped the back opening over it, settling the hat in place before knocking on the connecting door.

"Come in," Mark said.

When she entered, Larson was standing next to the door leading out into the hallway, and Mark was sliding his gun into the holster clipped at his waist. Both men wore jeans, sweatshirts marked with FBI on both the front and the back and hiking boots.

Mark's glance connected with hers in the mirror, but then he turned toward Larson, continuing their previous conversation. "Abe Rutherford's first two targets were small, only one or two casualties. It wasn't until he mastered his technique that he went after larger ones. Maybe our killer is doing the same thing. He could be a Rutherford fan."

Larson folded his arms in front of him. "So you think we should be looking for a connection between our killer and Rutherford?"

"And any environmentalist that Thesing was in contact with," Mark said. "I think we need to continue looking in all directions for the moment, until we have something that tells us otherwise."

As Mark grabbed the autoinjectors off the dresser and slid them into a case attached to his belt, Larson's speculative gaze settled on Beth. To avoid it, she checked her own weapon.

Eventually Larson gave up and shifted his attention to Mark again. "Command center is up and running over at the National Guard Armory now," Larson said as he opened the room door. Mark had ordered the change when it became apparent that the investigation not only needed more space, but also more security.

Five hours later the search party she'd been assigned to had walked nearly three miles into the forest, spaced ten feet apart and climbing steadily. Mark had divided the area to be searched into grids, assigning one to each of the seven teams. At that rate it would still take them a month to cover every square mile and didn't address the probability that, like Rutherford, their killer would continue to move around at night.

Beth paused to take a swig of water and to catch her breath. Despite the cold temperatures, she was beginning to perspire beneath the soft body armor and heavy sweatshirt. Starting out this morning, her leg muscles had been stiff. Once they'd loosened up some, though, she'd been fine. But within the last half mile or so, they'd started to cramp up on her. A condition that would become increasingly difficult to cope with and to hide.

Feeling Mark's gaze on her, she glanced over. He'd been keeping a close eye on her without ever getting too close.

And maybe it was better that way since she didn't know what she'd say to him, anyway. She was feeling overexposed at the moment. Wishing he'd never walked into her room last night. Wishing he hadn't seen her fall apart the way she did. And most of all, wishing that she could forget how when he'd kissed her this morning, she'd wanted him to stay.

But considering they were in the midst of what was quickly becoming one of the largest manhunts of all time, thinking about anything personal seemed wrong somehow.

She screwed on the cap to the water bottle. At least she didn't have to put up with Larson's scrutiny. Mark had assigned Larson the grid containing the roughest terrain, accessible only with the use of climbing gear and guts. The same twelve-square-mile area where Rutherford had disappeared for sixteen months.

It would take more than a day to hike in, and once there, the search party of nine agents and three local trackers would stay until they'd covered every square inch. And when they left, they'd leave behind surveillance equipment so the area could be remotely monitored.

As she was about to put away the water bottle, her cell phone went off. She recognized the Maryland area code, but not the number.

"Sleep well?"

At the familiar voice, her chest tightened with apprehension and her suddenly nerveless fingers dropped the bottle.

She looked for Mark, but didn't see him. Only a short distance from where he'd last been standing, though, were what the locals called rhododendron hells, an area where the bush was so thick it was nearly impenetrable. Making the assumption that he'd gone in to search it, she started walking toward the area.

"How did you get this number?"

"I'm not without resources."

He was mocking her. "That goes without saying. If you were, you wouldn't have the MX141."

"You did well yesterday. You're quite the jock."

"Not really. But still enough of one to nearly catch you." She was to challenge him at every opportunity. Not openly, but in a cautious, oblique manner that undermined his ego and put him on the defensive. The hope was that he'd reveal details about himself or about his plans.

He chuckled. "There's always next time."

She was nearly to the dense brush when Mark pushed his way out into the open again. Something in her face must have told him who the caller was.

"How did you know Harvey Thesing?"

Another soft chuckle. "We haven't even started playing yet, and you're already breaking the first rule of our little game."

"Then maybe you should fill me in. Let me know how it works."

"Rule number one. You ask too many questions, I hang up."

It was the one thing she couldn't allow to happen. Beth felt dread pool in her gut. "Agreed."

"What the hell do you think this is—a democracy?"

Because she didn't think he expected her to answer and she was afraid saying anything might piss him off, she remained silent.

"You've got this phone number in your caller ID. As soon as we're done talking, I'm going to take the battery out of this cell phone. But every few hours I'll put it back in for one minute. Just long enough for you to locate me. Do you understand?"

"Yes."

"Ever done any deer hunting?"

"No." Beth's gaze connected with Mark's. "I don't kill for the fun of it."

"Neither do I."

"Why do you kill, then?" She asked the question before she could stop herself and then waited the tensest split second of her life to see if he'd hang up.

"Because I can," he said, and she could hear the amusement in his voice. "Ever play connect the dots as a kid?"

"Yes."

"Well, that's what we're playing here. You connect them fast enough, you just might be able to stop me. If you don't, people die."

Chapter Fifteen

Mark already had the command center on the line when the killer disconnected. Grabbing her phone, he went to the incoming log. "I need to know the GPS coordinates of this cell phone number during the past few minutes, and I want it yesterday." As he read the number he realized that the area code was a familiar one. A Fredricks, Maryland, one.

Disconnecting and seeing just how pale Beth was, his inclination was to pull her into his arms. Instead, aware that they had an audience, he helped her to the closest tree.

"Sit with your back against the trunk."

After she slid down, he squatted in front of her, passed his own water bottle to her and waited while she took several sips.

"Okay. I need you to tell me everything he said."

They spent several minutes going over the conversation, the instructions she'd been given.

When his cell rang, he answered it. "What do you have?"

Mark knew the name of the agent on the end, but wouldn't have been able to put a face with it.

"He's at a truck stop just outside Atlanta, Georgia. The field office there is being contacted right now."

"And who is the phone registered to?"

"Harvey Thesing." The name didn't come as a surprise to Mark. When he'd seen the area code, he'd guessed as much.

"As soon as the local agents reach the truck stop, have them contact me."

While he'd been talking, Beth had climbed to her feet.

His gaze connected with hers as he closed his cell. He couldn't seem to stop himself from reaching out, but as soon as his fingers touched her cheek, she pulled back and turned her head slightly. With no other choice, he allowed his hand to drop again, recognizing that he owed her an explanation for his hasty retreat this morning.

He didn't know how he was going to provide one, though, since he couldn't fully explain it to himself.

At the time, he'd told himself it was because he wanted to protect her. Now he suspected there had been more to it. That, even more than protecting her, he'd been trying to protect himself. Not from any type of career fallout, but from something much more personal.

He'd been alone, a bachelor, for four years now, but had never felt particularly lonely. Until this morning. Until he'd pulled that door closed behind him.

"Come on, Benedict. It looks as if we're headed to Atlanta to start with."

It would take two and a half hours by car, but did they have that much time? How soon before the next *dot* was provided?

And how in the hell were they suppose to beat him there if they were always one step behind?

THE HIKE BACK took considerably less time because they were no longer looking for signs of the killer and because they were headed downhill. By the time they reached the staging area, a helicopter was waiting to take them to Atlanta.

Beth was pleased but surprised to see that Jenny Springer had been chosen to accompany them. The fourth agent riding with them was a member of the counterterrorism unit, Special Agent Dan Sturbridge. He was close to fifty and looked more like a marine than a special agent. She'd met him the first day, but she'd had little contact with him since.

As the pilot pulled open the door and motioned for them to climb in, Beth felt the first twinges of uncertainty. But it was nothing like what it usually was. The claustrophobia was getting better. Only a few weeks ago, she would have freaked just thinking about climbing into an elevator, let alone a helicopter.

Deep, slow breaths, Benedict.

She'd managed to survive the plane ride two days ago, hadn't she? But there had been a moment or two when if someone had handed her a parachute, she would have made use of it.

She felt a hand rest against her lower back. She looked up, her gaze meeting Mark's somber one. "You'll be fine."

She'd lost count of the times he'd said those words over the past few days.

With no other choice, she stepped aboard and, taking a seat, slipped on the headset that would allow them to communicate with one another during the flight.

As they lifted off, she looked down at the receding forest, recalling Mark telling her that he would take sixteen months without innocent lives being lost. Suddenly she wished the same and felt ashamed that she'd ever felt any differently.

Shifting her gaze, she caught sight of a news crew below, their camera aimed up at the helicopter.

Elvis has left the building.

Maybe now that the focus of the manhunt was elsewhere, the media would follow, leaving the people of Bellingham to begin the healing process. The helicopter gently swayed as the pilot turned it southwest.

Her heart might have missed half a beat and her breathing was on the quick side, but all in all, she was doing much better than she'd anticipated. Taking a deep breath, she held it for half a minute before letting it go.

"You know," Beth said, turning away from the view and focusing on Mark who sat across from her, "there's nothing to say that the unsub isn't in a helicopter right now or on a commercial flight to the West Coast."

Mark adjusted his mike. "If he's flying, it's not commercial. He needs to keep the chemical with him. Under current guidelines, it would have to go into checked luggage. He can't risk the airline losing his bag and putting him out of business. And as far as distance, he can't go too far. His game only works if we're close enough that we could conceivably catch him."

"Why the game, though?" Beth asked. "Why risk letting us get too close? Unless he wants us to stop him."

"I don't think that's what he wants. But we're not really going to know until we figure out why the Ravenels and why the school. Even if they were practice runs for him, they were still chosen for a reason. We figure that out and we start to figure him out." Mark glanced over at Jenny. "Did you turn up anything that connects Harvey Thesing and Abe Rutherford?"

"Several names came up, but I don't think they're going to be the break we're looking for. At least, not immediately. They're long-time activists. They donate heavily and they keep their governors and senators buried in letters. However, there's nothing that suggests any connection to a more extremist group. But to be on the thorough side, I contacted the field offices in their areas to do a more complete check of recent activities."

Dan Sturbridge flipped the mike into place. "One or two names on the dishonorably discharged military list also turned up on an antigovernment list. And a few were students of Richard Ravenel. Scott Duzenberry is tracking them down."

Beth retrieved her cell phone and upped the ring volume so she'd be able to hear it above the noise of the rotors. She'd given both her father and the unsub special ring tones.

The killer hadn't said he'd call. Only that he'd restore the battery in the phone so they could *see* him.

Stretching his feet out in front of him, Mark settled back in the seat. When their gazes met, she saw frustration in his eyes.

Having worked next to him for days now, she'd witnessed firsthand what it took to run this type of investigation. Not only great investigative skills, but management ones, too. And the ability to thrive under pressure.

But even Mark was feeling the strain of the past few days.

It hadn't been just days for him, though. He'd been working the case 24/7 for the past four months, ignoring his personal life.

Last night in the quiet darkness, he'd talked about his daughters. It was obvious that he loved them. And that he felt he'd let them down. Somewhere, laced within his words, had been an unspoken question. Should he leave the FBI? Shouldn't family come first? Before the country he'd taken an oath to protect and defend?

The fact that he grappled with those questions said a lot about the kind of man he was. The kind any woman would want beside her.

Beth turned and stared out the window.

THE HELICOPTER LANDED in Atlanta, Georgia, just over an hour and fifteen minutes later. A steady rain was already falling, but with the lower elevation, the temperature was ten degrees warmer than what they'd left behind in Bellingham.

Two SUVs were already waiting. Grabbing their luggage, they made the transfer in seconds.

Beth slammed the back gate closed. "I have the directions to the truck stop. Want me to drive?"

Mark had already pulled open the driver's door but now moved aside. Because he was on his cell phone, he gave a thumbs-up before walking around to the passenger side.

Saturday traffic was relatively light, so even with the wet road conditions they were making good time until they got to within several blocks of the truck stop.

Nothing looked very good beneath somber gray sky and drizzling rain, but the area they were in was obviously one of those in the early stages of flux.

The tightly packed, brick buildings lining both sides of the street looked old enough to be called historic. Some had For Sale signs out front, others had the trendy neon variety. Most of the businesses seemed to be the kind favored by first-time entrepreneurs: antique shops, an Internet coffee bar, an upholstery shop.

It definitely seemed like an unusual area for a truck stop.

Seeing the road block ahead, Beth started looking for a parking place. It was only then that she gave any thought to the second SUV and that it was no longer behind them.

But maybe Dan had known what kind of mess there was likely to be and had grabbed the first spot he'd found.

Mark was handling his ninth or tenth call now, this one about the ex-military angle. "Keep me posted." Disconnecting one call, he started to dial another. "You're a good driver, Benedict."

It was the second time today that he'd called her Benedict. First he'd left this morning without saying anything and now he was back to calling her Benedict. Seemed like a pretty clear indication of where things stood between them. She tried to tell herself that it was for the best, but couldn't quite ignore the sense of disappointment that settled in her chest.

Finally realizing that she wasn't going to find a space and that with vehicles crammed on both sides of the street, turning around was going to be difficult, she slammed the Explorer in Reverse, intending to back down the street until she found a spot. But as she shifted her foot off the brake and onto the gas, a fire truck came barreling in behind, siren going full blast.

With no other options, she jumped the curb in front of a coffee shop, forcing people to back out of her way.

As soon as the truck passed, she shifted the vehicle into Reverse.

Mark reached over and turned off the ignition. "No time for that. They're not going to be handing out any tickets today." Grabbing his baseball cap, he tugged it on.

Despite the worsening rain, people from nearby businesses continued to crowd the sidewalk. Mark and Beth hurriedly pushed their way through, ignoring the questions that flew at them from all sides. The sound of another siren could be heard above that of nearby interstate traffic.

Just before they reached the barricade, Mark's phone rang again. Answering it, he listened and then hung up without ever speaking. "Hazmat's on the scene. No fatalities and no indication yet that our guy used MX141. And Jenny and Dan are stuck out on the interstate, caught behind an accident. I told them to steer clear of here for the moment."

Holding his badge up for the patrol officer manning the barrier to see, Mark moved through the opening ahead of Beth.

The rain was coming down a bit more steadily now, and she could feel the dampness finally penetrating the sweatshirt and the T-shirt she wore beneath.

Crossing the street, they headed for Pete's Truck Stop. A semi had been backed up to the building, and men in full hazmat gear were carrying box after box of merchandise out of the store and loading it onto the truck. Every shelf would be cleared, each food item tested before being incinerated.

As they negotiated past the last set of barricades, the patrol officer pointed toward the front entrance of the building. "You'll find Special Agent Sheffield just around the other side."

Though Sheffield looked to be only in his late forties, his blond hair already showed silver streaks at the temples. After introductions, he gave them a rundown. "We've pulled the surveillance footage and collected the charge slips, but it'll take some time to obtain driver's license photos and do the eliminations."

Beth knew that even with a dozen agents working the eliminations, it would take at least five or six hours. And when they were done, they'd be left with the pictures of everyone who'd paid cash and maybe if they were extremely lucky, the killer's, too.

"After we evacuated, we interviewed the employees and any customers still on the lot, but nobody saw anything."

"Doesn't surprise me," Mark said, and Beth silently agreed.

"All I can say is your unsub either got lucky or he did his homework. This is the busiest stop in the area."

Mark's mouth flattened. "It wasn't luck."

Unfortunately, it appeared as if their guy may have gotten his act back together. If so, they couldn't count on any more slip-ups like yesterday morning.

"If you come up with anything, give me a call," Mark said.

"Will do."

Mark adjusted the baseball cap, pulling it even closer down over his eyes as they headed back to the SUV. "It's unlikely that our guy was stupid enough to get caught on surveillance tape or using a credit card. I think he's back in control."

Stopping, he glanced toward the interstate. "He didn't choose Atlanta just because of its size, he also chose it because within minutes of here, there are major highways going in every direction."

"So we can't even make an educated guess if he's heading north, south, east or west," Beth said.

Mark's mouth thinned as he glanced at his watch. "It's been over two hours. Assuming he's been moving the whole time, he has a two-hour lead on us right now.

"Two hours and growing."

Chapter Sixteen

Sitting on the sidelines waiting for the fight to be brought to him wasn't Mark's style.

One way or another they were going to have to find a way to throw the unsub off his game again.

Beth opened the back end of the SUV and then her suitcase, grabbing some clothes. "Give me a sec, I'm going to get out of this wet stuff." She tossed down her cap and started to peel off the sweatshirt.

Climbing behind the wheel, Mark retrieved the road map and spread it out in his lap. He tried to ignore what was going on behind the vehicle, but he couldn't quite keep his gaze from shifting to the rearview mirror.

The sweatshirt was already gone and she was tugging off her T-shirt. The bra beneath was the athletic type. When her gaze suddenly connected with his in the mirror, he didn't look away. She jerked on a dry T-shirt and then the sweatshirt. Grabbing her cap, she slammed the back gate and climbed into the passenger side.

Her mouth was set in a stiff line, and she had deep shadows under her eyes. And he couldn't quite forget the way she'd looked this morning asleep next to him. Or the way he'd left her so abruptly.

He started the car. "Let's grab some coffee and come up with a game plan of our own."

Mark's phone rang as he was putting the car in gear.

"We just got another coordinate for you, but this time the phone is staying active. And it doesn't appear to be moving."

He could think of only one reason why the killer would leave the battery in. Because time was up. And he wanted them to know it.

"Where," Mark asked.

"VerMar Beach. Florida's east coast. Just north of Palm Beach."

"He was just here in Atlanta two and a half hours ago. Start checking charter flights between Atlanta and South Florida. And book us seats on the next one out of Atlanta and headed anywhere close to VerMar Beach."

WITH THE ATLANTIC OCEAN on one side and the inner-coastal on the other side, the town of VerMar was a well-kept secret. A community of large estates hidden from public view behind tall, ornate fences and lush tropical plantings. It wasn't Palm Beach. It was the new playground of the well-heeled and indolent rich.

As soon as they turned onto Ocean Drive, the north-south boulevard that bisected VerMar, a local patrol officer stopped them.

Rolling down his window, Mark passed their badges. After scanning them, the officer handed them back. "It's Oceanside three miles down. You can't miss it."

Bellingham as a target had surprised Mark, but so, too, did VerMar. Mostly because they were at the opposite end of the socio-economic scale.

He glanced over at Beth. She didn't appear to be particularly wowed by the estates they passed, but then she'd been raised with money, so maybe they didn't seem quite so special to her.

"Do you like the beach?" he asked.

"Yes. And I like the water. Or at least I did before all this started. I haven't been able to take a shower without checking out the showerhead first. I suppose that makes me paranoid."

"No. That makes you normal."

He realized there were so many things that he didn't know about her. Things he wanted to find out when this was all through.

Turning into the elaborate entrance to Ocean Club, they were stopped again, their IDs checked before they were allowed to proceed.

The drive was long and winding. Royal palms lined the wide boulevard and were lit from beneath. The stiff breeze off the Atlantic shoved their fronds about.

Even before the SUV swept around the last graceful curve, he could see the flashing emergency lights ahead.

Fire trucks and ambulances and patrol cars were everywhere. And when every available square inch of pavement had been utilized, they'd resorted to using the St. Augustine grass. Mark followed suit. Getting out, he reached into the back seat and grabbed his hazmat gear.

"There's no reason for both of us to suit up." He sensed her relief. "Why don't you get a list of the guests? As soon as I check out the scene, we'll get started interviewing."

THIRTY MINUTES LATER Beth hit the play button, the screen on her laptop coming to life again.

Since she'd set up in a small meeting room where the

women members of the exclusive Ocean Club played bridge on Wednesdays and Fridays, she'd been systematically downloading and reviewing the videos taken by wedding guests. Until each of them could be interviewed, they'd been evacuated to the marina clubhouse.

Unlike some of the other recordings she'd viewed, the current one had been filmed by a more experienced hand. There was no jumping about, no shots of marble floors and feet or oversize crystal chandeliers.

She edged up the volume, but for the moment the only sound being picked up as the camera slowly panned around the main dining room was from the numerous conversations going on at nearby tables.

As a diplomat's daughter, Beth had seen plenty of beautiful rooms, but none had been any more elegant or refined than this one. It looked like something out of a Fitzgerald novel.

Dressed in gowns and tuxes, the guests were equally stylish and included several congressmen and the owner of a broadcasting network. Influential friends for an influential man. Senator Robert Wilkes, father of the bride, was well-known in Washington circles.

The scene suddenly changed, the lens now aimed at a pair of oversize French doors. Background noise faded as conversations dwindled to silence and people turned to face the opening.

Her chest tightened as she waited for what came next.

The doors were thrown wide, and the man holding the camera spoke for the first time. "And here comes the couple of the hour."

Beth's heart squeezed as Amanda and Nelson Peterson rushed into the room, smiling as if they'd just hit the lottery.

And from all appearances they had. They had it all, beauty, wealth and love.

Amanda was beautiful, a petite blonde with a large smile. Nelson was tall and dark and extremely handsome. They'd been holding hands the whole time, but now Nelson raised their clasped hands into the air. "Give it up for the most beautiful bride in the world." His smile was wide and as the camera came in for a close up, his eyes were filled with love and pride.

Today was to have been a beginning…

Pausing the film, Beth took a deep breath, preparing herself not to just watch the rest, but to study it closely, looking for additional clues.

She blinked away the tears that had collected despite her best attempts.

She'd come to know the other victims through crime-scene photos and from detailed but dry reports gathered by other agents. For the most part she'd been able to distance herself emotionally. But not this time. This time there was no isolating herself from any of the images caught by the camcorder—the joyful ones or the horrific ones.

Reading about what happened when MX141 came in contact with the human body was one thing, but watching it…

Nothing had prepared her for that. Or for the possibility that she was seeing her own death.

Her hands had been resting on the edge of the table, but looking down, she realized they had now curled into tight fists. How in the hell were they going to stop this guy? How many more people were going to have to die? And would she be one of them?

She looked up as Mark opened the door. Just seeing him made it easier for her to breathe, for her briefly to hide her fear.

Instead of entering, he lingered in the doorway, one hand on the doorknob, his broad shoulders filling the opening.

"How'd it go?" she asked. "Did you find the cell phone?"

"Yeah. As he was leaving, he tossed it in the bushes just outside the front doors. A local deputy found it."

"Why throw it away?"

"I don't know." His mouth thinned. "We'll be using the room across the hall to conduct interviews. I was going to get started with the senator, and have you talk to his wife in here. Miami is sending more agents to help with the interviewing. They should be here within the hour."

She nodded. "If you're going to be talking to the senator, I think you need to see this first."

He walked around the table and stopped next to her. "Then you found something?"

"Yeah. The other films I've reviewed stopped before this point."

Instead of sitting, Mark leaned down to watch, bracing one hand on the edge of the table and the other on the back of her chair. His nearness was enough of a distraction that she didn't hit Play immediately.

She felt his puzzled gaze on her, and then he reached past her and started the film from where she'd stopped it.

Instead of watching the screen, she studied him out of the corner of her eye. Even after everything they'd been through today, he still projected an amazing amount of energy and at the same time a level of competence that made it possible for her to believe they could actually win. That this killer could be caught.

That she might not meet the same end as the killer's most recent victim.

She found herself wanting to reach up, to run her hand

along his jawline, to feel the roughness and the warmth of his skin against her chilled hands. She recalled the way he'd held her last night, the way he'd made her feel safe and knew more than anything that was what she wanted to feel right now.

Forcing her thoughts away from him and back on the screen again, she watched as the camera followed the bride and the groom to the table of honor where the parents of both waited.

The groom's mother wasn't particularly beautiful and was nearly half a head taller than her narrow-shouldered husband, but they were old-moneyed Palm Beach.

The bride's parents were their polar opposites. Senator Robert Wilkes had come from a middle-class family and was tall, broad shouldered and darkly handsome. Mrs. Cindy Wilkes had been the reigning Miss Florida twenty-five years ago and looked as if she could still give this year's contestants a run for their money.

Despite their differences, both families seemed genuinely thrilled with the union of their children.

Mark shifted his stance as if impatient.

She tried to ignore the way her respirations had quickened. "It's coming up here soon. Watch the champagne glass."

It was only when the senator came to his feet somewhat unsteadily that it became apparent he'd already done too much celebrating and was well on his way to being drunk. And when he picked up a fork and loudly tapped it against the side of his water glass, disapproval blossomed on the faces of Cindy Wilkes and Gloria Peterson.

He smiled loosely as he reached for the champagne glass in front of him. "It's time for a toast—"

Amanda got to the glass first, though, and wrapping her

fingers around it, picked it up. "It's my turn to make a toast." She raised the glass. "To my new in-laws. Thank you for allowing me to be part of your family." She tipped the glass to her lips and sipped.

A stunned expression blossomed on her face. As she collapsed and started to convulse, Mark hit the stop button, his face grim. "The glass wasn't meant for her. The target was Senator Wilkes."

Chapter Seventeen

Beth could hear Cindy Wilkes screaming at her husband even before Mark opened the door to the room across the hall.

Robert Wilkes sat with his elbows propped on the table, head bowed, hands resting on either side of his head. To the untrained eye, he looked dejected, but the tension in his shoulders said otherwise.

Cindy Wilkes had her back to the door and was leaning across the table, her face only inches from her husband's. "It was our daughter's wedding day, for God's sake. Couldn't you stay sober for one goddamn day?"

Robert Wilkes' fingers slowly dug into his scalp like a man trying to claw something out of his brain. "What the friggin' hell are you saying?" His fists suddenly slammed onto the table in front of him, almost striking his wife's face. "That if I'd knocked back a few less bourbons, she'd be alive? That is friggin' bullshit!"

Seeing them, Robert Wilkes broke off and straightened.

Beth was amazed at how he managed to pull himself together. One second the politician was a man ready for a fight and the next he looked as if he was ready for Meet the Press. Cindy Wilkes was the exact opposite, once robbed of anger she seemed to shrink. As if that had been the only thing keeping her erect.

Mark motioned Beth into the room and then closed the door. "Actually, Senator, she would be alive. We have reason to believe that you were the intended target."

"What are you talking about? My daughter had a seizure. A heart attack. Something. I don't know." Suddenly he looked totally lost and completely alone.

"No, sir. Your daughter was poisoned. She came in contact with a chemical, a toxin."

"What in the hell are you talking about?" Throwing his shoulders back, the senator looked incredulous. "Why would anyone…"

"Maybe you both should sit down," Beth suggested and helped Cindy Wilkes into the chair next to her husband. After pouring and delivering a glass of water to the crying woman, Beth took a seat next to Mark.

Mark unzipped the soft-sided legal binder and pulled out a photo of Harvey Thesing. "Have you ever seen this man?" He placed it on the table.

Wilkes picked up the enlargement of Thesing's driver's license photo and studied it for several seconds. "Yeah. He was with Gil Carson at a charity event." Wilkes put down the picture.

"Do you mean lobbyist Gil Carson?" Mark asked. "The man who is currently under investigation?"

"Yes." Wilkes tapped at the center of the picture. "Gil Carson came up and pointed to this guy across the room and said this guy wanted to meet with me. I told him…I told Carson to get the hell away from me." Wilkes looked away. When he looked back, his jaw was set. "Tell me what in the hell is going on here?" He stabbed at the photo.

"Who in the hell is this man? What does he have to do with my daughter's…?" Looking away, he took a deep breath.

"He was a chemist," Mark said. "Employed by the lab where the chemical was developed."

"Developed for what?"

When Mark ignored the question, Wilkes wrapped his fingers around Mark's closest wrist. "I asked you a damn question!"

"And I'm asking you to remove your hand, sir."

After several seconds Wilkes let go and leaned back. "I have friends in high places."

"I'm sure you do, sir." Mark folded his hands over the portfolio. "What can you tell me about Carson? About his politics? And do you have any reason to believe he might want to harm you?"

"Seven or eight years ago he was one of the best lobbyists in Washington. Until he started seeing himself as a power broker and got greedy. When he did, doors started closing in his face."

"Yours included?" Beth asked. She hadn't been following the investigation closely, but knew that several members of congress were also under investigation.

Wilkes scraped his hands through his hair. "No. Not right away. Carson knew his stuff. Could present both sides. I continued to meet with him long after others on the Hill stopped. I figured that was my job. To listen to all sides before making a final decision. I always made it very clear that I vote my conscience."

Wilkes exhaled sharply. "Then around the middle of June I learned that Carson had approached a certain lawmaker, a close friend of mine and tried to buy his vote. This lawmaker's granddaughter had some major medical problems that insurance wouldn't cover. Carson was taking advantage of my friend's desperation. Long story short, my friend took the money. A week later, when he came to me, I counseled him to give it back. That if he didn't, Carson would own him. When this friend returned the money, Carson threatened him. Either he voted in favor of the environmental group or he'd be sorry."

Wilkes rubbed his bloodshot eyes. "I took what I knew to the authorities. A month ago Carson found out I was the one who blew the whistle on him."

"Did you ever socialize with him? Do you know anything about his background? Where he was from?"

"I used him for information and that was it. But I do remember his talking about being a military brat. That would have been when he was lobbying for a tank manufacture. Carson was a real apolitical chameleon. He'd represent anything as long as it paid well."

"So you don't think he's necessarily concerned about the environment?"

"No."

Could Carson be their man? Everything was strictly circumstantial, but there was enough of it to be fairly compelling.

Cindy Wilkes had been crying quietly, but now broke down in heaving sobs, her hands covering her mouth. She got to her feet. "You'll have to excuse me," she said, and headed for the door.

Concerned, Beth got up and followed her out, catching up to her in the hallway. "Mrs. Wilkes?" Beth said, touching the woman on her shoulder.

Turning, Mrs. Wilkes reached out. She wrapped her arms around Beth and held on tight, sobbing. Beth hugged her back, unsuccessfully trying to block out what she'd seen on the video tape. It had been difficult for her to watch. She couldn't imagine how terrifying it had been for this woman to actually be in the same room as it was happening. To watch her only daughter go into convulsions. To look into her daughter's frightened eyes and be able to do nothing.

Two special agents from the Palm Beach field office stood close by in the quiet hallway. They briefly looked at her but then turned away.

It was only a matter of a few minutes later that Robert Wilkes walked out, his expression grim, his posture slightly stooped. Looking up and seeing him, Cindy Wilkes backed away from Beth.

Beth would have liked to find the right words, but there really didn't seem to be any, so she settled for, "I'm so sorry about your loss."

Robert and Cindy Wilkes held on to each other as they walked toward the rear entrance. The couple only made it halfway to the doors before Cindy Wilkes suddenly crumbled at her husband's side. One moment he was trying to support her, to keep her on her feet, and the next they were both on their knees, holding on to each other, their shoulders heaving, their sobs filling the corridor.

Beth started toward them, uncertain what she'd do when she reached them, but unable to stand by and just watch.

Mark's hand on her shoulder stopped her.

Turning, he guided her away from them. He motioned to the closest special agent. "Give them some privacy, but stay with them at all times."

As she and Mark continued down the hallway, Beth looked over at him. "Did the Senator tell you anything else after I left?"

"When I mentioned the possibility that his friend might be the next target, he gave me his name. I'll make a call. Have him and his family picked up as a precaution."

"So you think it's Carson?"

Mark shrugged. "Maybe by morning we'll know more."

AS THEY WERE NEARING the lobby door, her cell phone rang. Hearing the ring tone—an old, nostalgic tune that she knew was her father's, she let it go to voice mail.

But almost immediately she regretted the decision. As Mark stopped to talk to the club manager, she excused herself and stepped just outside the nearest door. The night air was balmy, carried the scent of the nearby Atlantic.

Listening to Cindy Wilkes pour out her heart and her grief had made Beth realize that even if her father was in the wrong, even if he wasn't always an easy man, he was still her father. As she'd told Mark the other night, she and her father would eventually get past everything.

But at what cost? How much time would they have lost? And what if something did happen to her...?

Beth dialed her father's number. When he answered, she said, "I couldn't get to my phone. I'm sorry."

"No. I'm the one who is sorry. About the way I've been interfering. I know how much your career means to you, but..."

"You were worried. I know." It was the first time in her memory that her father had apologized. Usually they somehow managed to make up without either of them taking blame.

"You okay?" he asked, and she could hear the concern in his voice.

"I'm fine."

"How's the new assignment going?"

She rubbed her eyes. "Is it okay if we don't talk about work right now?"

"Sure."

Beth wandered a few steps from the door. "You remember how much Mom liked the beach? How we'd take flashlights after dark and walk along it? Looking for those little crabs that scurry around at night?"

"And the way she would collect shells? I just came across a box of them the other day." Beth could hear the emotion piling up in his voice and felt her own chest tighten.

"Were you searching for something?"

"No. I was looking… I was…" There a sense of loneliness not just in his voice but in the statement, too.

Had he been digging through cabinets and closets, hoping to stumble on something that would remind him of her mother?

Turning back, she saw Mark still talking to the manager. He lifted his chin, indicating that he knew where she'd gone.

Her father cleared his throat. "Beth?"

He'd obviously thought they'd been disconnected. "I was thinking. Maybe we could go someplace warm this Christmas. A beach somewhere."

There was a pause where it was her turn to wonder if they'd been disconnected.

"I'd like that," he said simply, but she could hear the emotion in his voice. Why hadn't she understood just how hard the past two years had been on him, too? To lose her mother to cancer and then almost immediately to lose Beth when she'd gone undercover.

"I'll call you soon and we'll talk about it, okay?"

"That sounds fine."

"I need to go." She glanced over her shoulder, checking on Mark again.

"Okay," her father said. "But do me a favor."

"Sure. What?"

"Save the world if you have to, but take care of yourself at the same time."

"I will. And I love you," she said as she ended the call, but she wondered if he'd heard her.

When her phone rang almost immediately, she knew it wasn't her father calling back, but assumed it would be one of the other agents.

"We've both had a very busy day, haven't we?"

At the sound of his voice, her fingers tightened on the phone and adrenaline surged through her. She wasn't ready to handle this bastard. Not so soon after watching a woman die on her wedding day. Not after witnessing the grieving parents deal with the horror of their daughter's senseless death and watching a strong man brought to his knees as he realized that he had been a target. That the daughter he so obviously loved had lost her life because of him.

"Go to hell!" She hung up on the bastard. Almost immediately, the phone rang. She let it go to voice mail, but it wasn't more then five seconds before it was ringing again. This time she answered it. "I'm flattered. You obviously have me on speed dial."

"Bitch. Don't do that again. No one hangs up on—"

She disconnected, expecting him to call right back. When he didn't she started to worry that she'd screwed up, that her decision to shake up the power dynamic between them had been a wrong one. But she'd had to do something. Acting like a lamb being led to slaughter, meekly accepting his rules and cautiously challenging him hadn't really gotten them any closer to catching him.

Beth glanced back inside to where Mark was still talking to the local police chief and several security officers for the resort. What was she going to tell him if the bastard didn't call back? There was no way that she could whitewash what she'd just done. She had disobeyed a direct order not to openly challenge the bastard.

Then she realized that she was worrying about the wrong thing. That for the moment at least she needed to consider how she was going to handle things if the bastard did call back. Turning her back to the glass wall again, she stared down at the cell-phone screen. Apologizing was out of the question. It would show too much desperation on her part. Was the man on the other end Carson? And if it was, how would he react if she used his name? She decided against it, though, almost immediately. For the moment, if this was Carson, he had no idea that they were on to him.

Maybe she should just treat him like any other man who had called her a bitch. There would be nothing challenging in the stance, and at the same time, she wouldn't really be backing down.

She was still working out her strategy when the call came in. On the second ring she answered it. "No one calls me a bitch." She was careful to keep her voice neutral. There was a fairly long pause while she waited. Had she just made yet another miscalculation? If he hung up now…

"I bet the videos made for some interesting viewing. Think maybe I could get a copy?"

She exhaled, the tightness in her chest easing despite his request. "Sure. Just stop on by, and I'll have one ready for you. And a pair of handcuffs to go with it."

"The spoiler of fun."

As it had in all the previous calls, his voice carried an edge of amusement. This time she didn't find it quite so unsettling. "What is it that you want?"

"Conversation. Someone to share all the highlights of the trip with." He chuckled softly. "Solitary vacations are such a bitch, don't you think?"

A vacation? "Perhaps you shouldn't have killed your partner, then."

He ignored her observation, instead returned to an earlier thread. "Think I could get a copy of the photos you guys took at the farmhouse for my vacation scrapbook?"

"Tell me why you chose that family, and I'll think about it."

"That's okay. I took my own. If you're not in any hurry for them, I could e-mail a set when my itinerary isn't quite so full." He chuckled. "For now, though, you better rest up."

The idea that he'd gone back in to take photos sickened her, but she couldn't let it show. "Why's that?"

"Because tomorrow starts a new game. New stakes. New rules." As he paused, she could hear the piano in the background. "So good night, Beth, and pleasant dreams."

The line went dead.

New game. New rules. New stakes. As she started to lower the phone, she felt someone standing right behind her.

"I assume that was our guy again?" Mark took the phone from her. As she started to fill him in, he checked the number.

She could have lied to protect herself, not fully disclosing how she'd handled the call, but this wasn't really about her, about keeping her job. It was about stopping a killer.

Mark's expression turned troubled as he listened. He'd

trusted her. She'd let him down. And in the process had possibly put countless lives at risk.

"I'm sorry. I know I shouldn't have but—"

"Don't apologize for making the right decision. You've got him talking now, seeing you as a confidante of sorts."

His hands closed over her shoulders, his thumbs brushing across her collarbone. "What you need is to get some rest. Which is what you're going to do right now. I arranged for a bungalow. There was only one available, but it has a separate bedroom. You can have the bed. I'll take the couch."

If she hadn't been so damn scared, she might have seen the irony in his worrying about where they'd sleep. They'd already shared a bed. And she doubted either of them would be getting much sleep tonight no matter where they laid their bodies.

LIKE THE REST of the property, the bungalow was beautiful, but much more casual than the main building. The floors and ceilings were heart pine, the furniture covered in white duck slip covers. Large shells and nautical items filled the bookshelves in the living room. A small morning kitchen outfitted with a coffeemaker and a small stainless steel refrigerator was tucked just outside the bedroom.

The wall facing the ocean was floor-to-ceiling glass, and because it was dark outside, she saw her reflection. Beth tightened her arms in front of her and turned away. The wild-haired woman with the too-big eyes didn't even look like her.

Walking into the bedroom and seeing more large windows, she immediately closed the drapes.

When she returned from the bedroom door, Mark was

setting up his laptop on the desk in front of the living room window.

"If you don't mind, I think I'll catch a shower," she said and grabbed her suitcase.

Thirty minutes later when she walked out of the bedroom, he was reviewing another of the wedding videos. Not on the laptop, but on the large plasma television. Seeing her, he turned it off.

His feet were propped on the ottoman in the center of the seating area, and he looked oddly at ease. Or maybe it was that she was anything but relaxed.

He lifted a wineglass. "I opened some wine. It's there on the counter."

Any other time she would have had a glass or two to calm her nerves, but when he'd lifted the glass it had reminded her too much of Amanda proposing a toast.

Chapter Eighteen

Less than an hour later, Beth climbed into the kingsize bed, but within ten minutes she was up again, standing at the large window, staring out at the beach. Even with the thick glass, she could hear the harsh surf as it crashed against the sand. The clouds riding the horizon flirted with the rising moon. Last night she'd watched it breach a mountain, tonight it was the ocean that it rose above.

She glanced at the bed with longing. She was so tired, so desperate for sleep, but every time she'd closed her eyes, her mind replayed in panoramic detail the last moments of Amanda's life. The horror, the incomprehension in her eyes and in the eyes of everyone around her.

A new game, with new stakes and new rules.

She couldn't quite block out the fear that she could be next. That no matter how strong she was or how determined Mark was, it wouldn't be enough. Just before she'd retreated to the dark bedroom, he'd received a preliminary report on Carson as well as a photo. She'd read the report, but refused to look at the picture, afraid that his face, too, would rob her of sleep.

Her shoulders jerked as a razor-sharp shiver climbed

through her body. She wasn't chilled, though, she was frightened. If only she could shut it out for one whole night. If only she could find a dreamless sleep.

It had been over two years since she'd felt safe. Since she'd felt naively invincible. She wondered if she'd ever feel either of those things again.

Hearing the bedroom door open behind her, she turned. Mark stood in the doorway. Seeing her there, he walked toward her.

"I thought I heard you up."

"Just restless." They both knew she was lying.

As he wrapped his arms around from behind, pulling her back against his lean body, the moon suddenly broke free of the distant cloud cover. Whitecaps that had been barely visible before turned almost iridescent.

"Beautiful moon, isn't it?" Mark murmured next to her ear, his warm breath stirring her hair.

"A hunter's moon. That's what the ranger you sent to get me last night called it."

Mark's body tensed behind her. Even before he turned her to face him, she knew something was wrong but couldn't understand what.

His fingers tightened on her shoulders. "When was this?"

"When I walked over to the restroom—"

"I didn't send anyone looking for you."

She swallowed against the lump of fear that grew in her throat. It wasn't possible. Was it? She looked up into his face. "I need to see Carson's photo."

She followed him back into the living room. As soon as he ran his finger over the touch pad, the face came into focus.

He'd stayed mostly in the shadows, but she still recognized the face.

"Beth?"

Her fingers curled at her side.

"That's him. That's the man. I stopped to look at the moon, and he stepped out of the trees. He was wearing a forest ranger's jacket." Last night she'd stood within five feet of the man they hunted. She rubbed her forehead. How could she have been so stupid? "I sensed something wasn't right, but I kept telling myself that I was imagining it."

Carson could have taken her then. When she'd turned her back to walk away. Why hadn't he? Why had he let her go? Why had he let her believe that she was clever?

With a grim expression, Mark pulled her into his arms. This time she wrapped hers around him and held on tight, as if as long as she did, she'd be safe.

She didn't cry. It was as if she was so numb that she couldn't anymore. As if she'd been frightened for so long that it no longer registered.

"Come morning, you're going somewhere safe." His arms tightened around her. "Until this is over. Somewhere I won't have to worry about him finding you. He's no longer a ghost. We have a name now. Agents are already on their way to his home. In another few hours we'll be able to track his credit card use."

He wanted to send her someplace safe. Because he cared about her. Come morning, she'd argue with him, make him see that she'd be safer with him than she would be anywhere else. But for tonight she wanted to forget everything. Needed to feel something besides the aching cold inside her.

As she reached up and ran her fingertips over his lips, he went stock-still. His eyes narrowed slightly and his breathing turned slightly irregular. She could feel the tension radiating from his body. Felt her pulse kick a little harder in response. She'd never tried to seduce a man. At least not one like Mark.

His firm chest was only inches from her. She lowered her lips kissing him there, trailing her lips upward to press yet another kiss at the hollow of his throat. As she looked up at him this time, his hand slid from her shoulder upward, his thumb tracing the side of her neck and then her jawline. When he reached the back of her neck, he drew her to him, angling her lips up to his.

He kissed her slowly at first, taking his time, tasting the corners of her mouth. And then suddenly, as if he couldn't stop himself, he deepened the kiss. Her lips opened beneath his, wanting more.

His hand had been resting at her hip for nearly a minute, but now moved upward, taking the hem of her T-shirt with it. Cool air reached her exposed skin, but it was the warmth of his hand that made her shiver. Made her want more. And when he finally reached a breast, she arched into the caress. Her breath caught and then escaped in a rush as he gently teased the tip, the sensation settling at her very core.

He lifted his lips from hers but didn't pull away, his warm breath brushing across them still. "Are you sure?" His voice was tight and slightly raspy.

"I'm sure."

He turned and led her into the bedroom where moonlight pooled down onto the floor but didn't quite reach the bed.

She sat on the edge, expecting him to follow her down, but he didn't. Instead, he dropped to his knees in front of her, leaning in to slowly kiss her again. Easing back slightly, he pushed her T-shirt up slowly, exposing her. She tugged it the rest of the way, dropping it among the sheets as his warm mouth closed over the tip of one breast.

Her muscles seemed to melt, and as his lips and tongue and teeth moved over her, her hands ran through his short dark hair.

When she didn't think she could stand anymore, he pushed her gently backward. As he did, she reached for him, wanting to bring him with her, wanting to feel the weight of his body covering hers.

But he didn't. Instead, he teased down her boxer shorts, his lips and tongue exploring each exposed inch. As the light stubble along his jaw rasped her inner thigh, she couldn't bite back the soft moan that built at the back of her throat. And when, a second later, his warm breath brushed against her very core, her body arched. There was magic in those movements. Delicious magic.

And then he was on the bed with her, stretched out beside her, no longer wearing the sweatpants. Turning her face to his, he kissed her softly as one hand followed the line of her hip. As his fingers touched her between the thighs, they parted. He continued to kiss her as his fingers stroked, then circled slowly and then probed, dragging sensations out of her that she'd never felt before.

Reaching down, she stilled his hand, stopping the magic. "I don't want to be the only one," she said, her breath unsteady, her skin slick and on fire. She reached for him and ran her hand upward along his length, feeling the heat and the power.

He pulled her lips to his again, his mouth moving over hers with desperation now, his breathing just as uneven as her own.

He shifted over her, his gaze connecting with hers as he pushed slowly into her, the stretching heat as he filled her briefly robbing her of breath.

He looked down at her, his gaze intense, and then lowered his lips until they were all but touching hers. "You're beautiful," he murmured.

He began to move. Slowly at first, with firm but gentle strokes that she rose up to meet. Then he thrust harder and harder still, filling her with a maddening mixture of pleasure and need.

Within minutes his breathing tightened as he fought to postpone his surrender. And she could feel her own building deep inside her. Could feel her body reaching for the ultimate release. She wrapped her legs around him, dragging him into her, wanting all of him. Needing all of him.

Starting deep inside her, hot pleasure shot through her body. She arched up, a harsh moan being torn from deep inside her as she started to come.

His rhythm changed and he thrust hard and deep, his breathing as ragged as her own now as he pushed her over the edge. As soon as he had, his thrusts slowed. And then she felt the subtle jerk of his body, the heavy throbbing deep inside her.

Leaning over her, breathing hard, Mark's lips and teeth teased her chin. "There isn't anything about you that isn't sexy as hell."

He seemed to study her face intently for several seconds before his eyes narrowed. Suddenly lowering his head, he pressed his forehead to hers.

For several minutes, because they were so busy catching their breaths, neither one of them spoke or moved again. And then suddenly he rolled to the side, taking her with him. He dragged the sheet up over them and pulled her in tight.

And for the first time in years she felt safe.

Chapter Nineteen

It was still the middle of the night when Mark slipped out of bed and pulled on sweats.

Crossing to the window, he looked out at the night. The moon was high now. A hunter's moon. A cold sense of unease settled in his gut just thinking about what could have happened last night. How close Carson had been able to get to her.

Why risk it, though? Because he felt empowered? Because he believed himself unstoppable? Or because he hadn't been able to stop himself? Because even stronger than the desire to kill was the need to be near Beth?

If the latter was true, no place was going to be safe until Carson was in custody.

Hearing her stir, he was tempted to strip and join her once more beneath the covers. To make love one more time before letting reality intrude.

He slowly rubbed the back of his neck. What in the hell was he going to do? There was no going back, pretending that tonight had never happened. But was there any way for them to move forward? He'd been a loner for four years now. The thought no sooner flowed through his mind than he recognized the underlying fallacy. It hadn't been just four years, it had been a lifetime. Even during eight years of marriage, he'd always held something back.

So what made him think he could change now? That he could open up with even Beth. Because she made him want that level of intimacy more?

He stared down at her. What made him think that he could give her what she needed? He tugged the sheet over her bare shoulder. His fingers curled as his hand dropped away.

Leaving her, knowing that he wouldn't be able to sleep, he turned on the computer out in the living room and opened the report that had been e-mailed to him during the past few hours.

While he'd been making love to a woman under his command. It wasn't a hanging offense maybe, but it was a punishable one.

Closing his mind to that line of thought, he started reading the report.

Carson had already been under investigation for tax evasion, fraud and conspiracy to bribe a public official, so there had been quite a bit of background information going in. The late-night search and several key interviews had turned up some additional insights into the man.

Just over four months ago, Carson had learned he had terminal cancer. And recently he'd been prescribed some heavy duty pain medication.

First legal problems, then the medical kind and finally financial ones. All of Carson's recent troubles had added up to a drained bank account. Which led to the most promising break for them. Unable to access any cash, he'd been forced to use credit cards that could be easily tracked. And that wasn't the only good news. Even though it wasn't turned on at the moment, there was a cell phone registered to Carson. Over the past few weeks, three calls had been logged to a Maryland oncologist, suggesting that Carson kept the phone with him.

Between the credit cards and the cell phone, they should be able to take him down—unless he found out they were on to him. If he did, they'd be worse than screwed. For the moment Carson felt invisible. Once he realized he wasn't, there was no way to predict how he would react. Especially considering that he wasn't just a military brat, he'd also spent several years in Special Forces. He'd received an honorable discharge shortly after the Gulf War, but some of the wording in the transcripts suggested that may have been because his father, a thirty-year decorated veteran, had called in some favors.

The next area ran through Carson's life chronologically, much of the information compiled using information on the father's military career. Gil Carson had been born in Arizona. The first move had taken him to Fort Hood in Texas. The location rang a bell with Mark. Harvey Thesing had never joined the military, but his mother had been an army mechanic. Mark grabbed the Thesing file, locating the section that dealt with the chemist's early background. Twenty-two years ago, Thesing's mother and Carson's father had been stationed at the same base. Was it possible that they had met there?

But why hadn't Carson's name come up on the list of known associates for Thesing? Because they hadn't had contact during the interim? Come morning, Mark would have agents from the closest field office check it out more thoroughly.

Mark refocused on the Carson report. When Carson had

been seventeen, he'd been sent to live with an aunt just outside Bellingham. He'd attended the high school for less than a month before withdrawing to be home schooled. Mark rubbed his forehead. Richard Ravenel would have been the basketball coach during that time. But it seemed unlikely that the problem between them could have had anything to do with basketball or school.

Which left what?

Mark retrieved the soft-sided briefcase propped against the desk and grabbed out the Ravenel file. Livengood had said the daughter had died from some type of hunting accident. Believing it unrelated to the current situation, Mark had only scanned the report. He now read it much more closely. Because the shooting had taken place during deer season and in an area frequented by hunters, it had been ruled a hunting accident, but no one had ever been charged. A .306 round had obliterated the young woman's chest. There'd been nothing left of Kim Ravenel's heart.

He checked the date. Carson had still been in Bellingham at the time. Mark scanned back through the Carson report again, locating the date he'd joined the army. It was less than a week after the girl's death. Coincidence? Or was it possible that Kim Ravenel had been Gil Carson's first victim?

Had Kim spurned Carson's advances? Or considering that Carson had returned years later to kill the rest of the family, maybe Richard Ravenel had forbidden his daughter from seeing Carson? Or maybe, like the rabbit that Carson had left behind that day, maybe even at seventeen he liked to kill.

As Mark read the next paragraph, a sense of extreme

unease set in. Three weeks after Gil Carson's discharge from the military, his father had been killed in a hunting accident.

Mark was no longer wondering if Gil Carson was responsible for two murders, he was now wondering just how many others Carson had killed.

Flipping to the last page of the Ravenal report, Mark felt his lungs shut down. The young woman's face staring back at him bore a striking resemblance to Beth.

If he'd been having second thoughts about sending Beth away, he no longer did.

As he had pointed out earlier, they had a name now. Ways to track this killer. She'd risked enough already. Deep down inside, he knew none of those was the real reason he was pulling her off this investigation, though. It was because he didn't want to see anything happen to her, and realizing that brought into focus just how much she meant to him.

Booting down the computer, he headed back to bed. For a few more hours he could hold her in his arms. Could hold tomorrow at bay.

JUST AFTER 6:00 A.M. he sat in the living room with his cup of coffee.

The sun was a peachy-orange spill of light at the horizon, the ocean calmer than it had been last night. And in many ways, he felt calmer, too. More focused.

He'd found an extra blanket and pillow and had made up the couch to look as if he'd slept there and not with Beth. Better to maintain the illusion at least.

He picked up his cell phone and dialed Traci's number. Maybe it was a bit early, but he was afraid if he didn't make the call now, things would get crazy again, and he wouldn't get the chance.

She answered on the fourth ring, her voice husky with sleep.

"Hi," he said simply. "I know it's early, but I was hoping we might be able to talk."

"Okay," she said, her voice soft and somewhat indistinct. "Let me just wake up a bit here."

"Maybe while you do, I could just talk. Spill my guts a little bit."

"Sure."

"I've been thinking a lot about Gracie, about what she's going through. And thinking about what I put you through those last few years. You're right. I was never there. It wasn't because I didn't want to be. But I know that needs to change. When I put this current investigation to bed, I'm going to make some changes."

"Is the investigation you're working on right now more important than your daughter crying herself to sleep at night?"

That was such a tough question. One that there was no real answer for. "Nothing is more important to me than Gracie and Addison. But we all have to make sacrifices."

"They're children, Mark, they shouldn't have to make too many of them. They only get one childhood. You only get one opportunity to see them grow up."

He wiped a hand down his face. "I'm just asking you to hold off talking to the lawyers for a few more days. Until this is behind me. Can you do that for me?"

There was a long pause, sounds of covers being kicked aside.

"Can you do that for me?" he asked again.

"Yeah. We don't have to make any decisions right now."

He heard the old four-poster bed squeak. "We need to

talk about something else, too. I've been dating this man for about six months now, and…"

He was about to ask why he hadn't been told but then realized that if he'd been around more, he would have known. "Is it serious?"

"Yes. We haven't set a date yet."

"Is he a good guy?"

"Yeah. You're going to like him."

BETH SPENT MORE TIME blow drying her hair and getting dressed this morning than she had the previous one. Partly because she wouldn't be tramping around a forest and partly to give herself time to think about what had happened last night. To sort out her feelings some. She was in love with Mark Gerritsen. There was no longer any way she could deny it. Three years ago when she'd been his student, she'd fallen in love with the bigger-than-life idea of Mark Gerritsen, but over the past few days she'd fallen in love with the man himself.

But was there any reason to believe he felt anything?

And if he didn't… What would she do then?

When she stepped out into the living room, Mark was just getting off the phone. Looking up, he smiled.

"You look beautiful."

"Thanks." She poured herself a cup of coffee. When she stopped next to where he was sitting in the desk chair, he took the cup from her and placed it next to his before pulling her onto his lap. He gave her a very leisurely kiss.

Pulling back slightly, he smiled. "Good morning."

She was smiling, too, now. But then, out of the corner of her eye, she noticed the blanket and pillow on the couch.

Why go to the trouble to make it appear as if he'd slept out here? Unless he was expecting company…

He started to kiss her again, but this time she moved backward slightly, withholding her lips. Her eyes narrowed. "What's going on?"

His hold briefly tightened, but then, possibly feeling her stiffen in his arms, he released her. "We need to talk."

She moved away nervously, taking her coffee with her. When she'd put enough distance between them, she faced him. "Talk about what?"

Mark's mouth thinned and his expression became shuttered again. The way it was most of the time. Except when he gave good-morning kisses and when he was deep inside her. Beth put down the cup and folded her arms in front of her.

"Larson's on his way over," Mark said. "He's going to be putting you on a plane this morning."

"Why are you doing this?"

Clasping his hands in front of him, he looked up at her, his mouth set in a hard line. "Why do you think?"

"Because you're putting my safety in front of this country's?"

He didn't argue. Maybe she should have taken some comfort in the idea that he did care about her. That maybe he'd been feeling some of the same things this morning that she had been. But she didn't. Because she knew in the end, if another person died because of the decision, he would find it difficult to live with himself.

He'd briefly looked away, but his gaze now met hers. "We have a name now and a credit card trail to follow. With other ways to track him, there's no longer any reason for you to continue putting yourself in that kind of risk. And as your supervisor, doing anything that puts you need-lessly in danger…" He rubbed his mouth.

She could tell that even he wasn't buying what he was trying to sell her. "But you still need me."

He remained mute. A knock sounded at the front door. "That'll be your ride."

"So that's it?"

"Yes."

As Mark let Larson in, she shoved her clothes into the suitcase and gathered up the toiletries she'd left in the bathroom.

She offered a tight nod to her escort. "When did you arrive?"

"Couple of hours ago." Larson gave Mark a quizzical look, his gaze briefly scanning the couch and then the two of them. It was obvious that he knew that Mark hadn't slept out here, but he didn't say anything. Instead, he picked up her suitcase.

As she was about to follow him out, Mark grabbed her by the upper arm, tugged her away from the opening. He kissed her fast and hard and thoroughly. Pulling back, he studied her face. "Keep yourself safe."

She was afraid to speak, afraid of what might spill out of her mouth, so offered a slight nod.

When she stepped outside, Larson was just tossing her suitcase in the backseat. Instead of pulling the dark sedan in, he'd backed it in.

The morning was cooler than she'd expected, the air heavy with moisture and a briny scent. Not even a foot from the bungalow's door and she already felt sticky. As if she'd spent an hour walking the beach.

Larson's cell phone rang. Backing away from the car,

he answered it as she slid into the passenger side. She was clicking her seat belt across her when she heard the choked-off grunt and the sound of a body dropping.

Before she could react, a man wearing an FBI hat…Carson…slid into the driver's seat and reached for the ignition. She wondered if the hat was hers. If he'd found it in the restroom.

The seat belt blocked easy access to her weapon. She went for the SIG-Sauer anyway. But before her fingers reached it, she felt the icy-cold contact of a gun barrel at her temple.

"If you move, I'll put a bullet in your head right here and now."

She studied his face out of the corner of her eye. He looked like a man who was barely holding on. She couldn't see the weapon he held to her head, or even the finger resting against its trigger, but she saw the way his arm shook slightly.

She slowly lifted her hands, indicating she'd do as he asked.

As soon as she did, Carson punched the accelerator, the rear tires of the sedan flinging gravel everywhere.

Chapter Twenty

As soon as she walked out the door, as soon as Mark heard it close behind her, he started second-guessing himself. Had he made the right decision? Was sending her away the right thing to do?

Reaching the window overlooking the beach, he stared out at the deserted stretch of sand, admitting that what he really wanted to do was take her away himself.

That hadn't been an option, though. He had a job to finish.

And then something hard rained against the front door. Not even taking the time to identify what had caused it, he ripped open the door just in time to see the shadow of the dark Taurus disappear down the heavily landscaped lane.

He brought up the automatic, but never got a chance to get off the first shot.

Cursing, he lowered his weapon. He was just as likely to hit Beth as Carson.

Dropping down next to Larson, he checked for a pulse, thought that maybe he felt one. Leaving the bungalow's door standing wide open, he jumped into the SUV. As he negotiated the drive, he called for an ambulance. There was nothing he could do for his friend right now.

He sped past the guard gate, nearly running down the security guard who'd been foolish enough to try to stop him. How in the hell had Carson managed to get by security? Since last night, the Ocean Club had been crawling with both private security and public law enforcement.

Hitting the main road, he paused. Which way? Knowing that any hesitation ate up important seconds, he turned right, praying that he was right.

Mark placed a call, requesting GPS coordinates for Beth's cell, and then waited tense minutes for a response.

The agent on the other end gave him the coordinates, and he set the navigation system. His fingers tightened on the steering wheel. "Now I need someone to check recent activities on Gil Carson's charge cards. And Special Agent Beth Benedict's, too."

Accessing credit card activity would take time, maybe more than they had.

Up until now Carson had seemed to prefer areas with enough traffic that he could get himself lost among it. To the right was VerMar's small downtown area with quaint shops. But nothing would be open at this time of morning. But Carson's behavior suggested that he was beginning to unravel. Wasn't thinking as clearly as he had been in the beginning.

This morning's kidnapping was a good indication of just how far he'd gone in the downward spiral. For months he'd managed to avoid detection. He'd pulled off the school killings without anyone ever seeing him. And it would have been the same at the Ravenel place if he hadn't made the 911 call.

But he hadn't been able to stop himself.

Just as he hadn't been able to stop the blitzkrieg-style attack this morning. An organized offender would never have attempted it. Too many variables. No way to control any aspect of the situation.

Mark's gut instincts had told him that Carson was falling apart. That Carson was about to make his big move. Mark just hadn't expected it quite so soon. But he should have.

A new game with new stakes and new rules.

Because Mark had gotten sloppy, Beth was very possibly going to die. With Carson's current legal and medical problems and his ex-military background, it was unlikely that he'd allow himself to be taken alive.

Maybe the only ace they held at the moment was that Gil Carson had no idea they now knew his identity.

BETH GLANCED OVER at Carson. He'd shaved within the past forty-eight hours maybe, but not within the past twenty-four, and it looked as if he'd slept in his clothing.

Shifting her gaze downward without moving her chin, she saw the sand covering the floor mat. Was that how he'd gotten by security? By using the beach?

The gun he held on her was a nickel-plated .357.

He was being forced to split his attention between her and the road. She recalled the driver's license photo. The well-groomed appearance. The clean-shaven face. The neatly combed blond hair. This man looked as if he'd spent the night drunk on the beach, sleeping among the crabs and seaweed. And he didn't smell much better, either.

What about Larson? Was he hurt, or was he dead? And did anyone, did Mark know that Carson had her? If not…

"I said, undo your safety belt, Beth."

As she started to reach down with her left hand, she realized it was shaking uncontrollably. It wasn't just adrenaline this time. She was damned scared. Her fingers curled hesitantly as she tried to get control of her fear. She needed to stay calm.

"Now, Beth!"

She pushed on the release button. Pulled her hand out of the way as the belt retracted across her. Her weapon would be next. When it came to holding a gun, she was ambidextrous, could use either hand. He wouldn't know that. Could she use it to her advantage?

"Now the gun! I want you to reach across with your right hand and very slowly, using only two fingers, I want you to remove it. No sudden moves."

Fear pooled in her chest again, her breathing going shallow as she considered what her next move should be. And then she remembered that the weapon in her holster wasn't her usual one, didn't have an ambidextrous safety. That she'd had to turn over the weapon she normally carried after the garage shooting. And there was no way she'd be able to get a left-handed safety off with her right hand quickly enough.

With no choice, using the thumb and index finger of her right hand, she carefully lifted her weapon free of the holster. Once it was gone, there would only be her cell phone left.

The window beside her slid down silently, the wind screaming inside. Carson had originally taken the same road as she and Mark had used last night, but had since made a number of turns. They were now on a straight stretch of roadway with some type of crop field on either side and no signs of development.

"Toss it, Beth!"

She complied.

"Now your phone."

She unclipped it from her belt, but then fumbled it. It dropped down between the door and the seat. The butt of Carson's weapon slammed into the side of her head with enough force that she was momentarily disoriented. Pain radiated through her skull.

"That was very stupid. Either you find the cell phone now, Beth, or you get a bullet in the head!"

Having seen Amanda Wilkes's death, getting shot didn't sound so bad. But she shoved her hand into the space repeatedly to buy time to sort out her options. The phone might be the only way that Mark would be able to find her. And more importantly stop Carson.

"I'm not bluffing here, Beth. If I have to stop this car to get that phone, they'll find you in a ditch with six rounds in your skull."

His constant use of her name was beginning to bother her. As he took a curve too fast, the momentum shifted the phone enough that it bumped into her fingers.

Should she pick it up?

She didn't doubt that if she didn't come up with it fairly soon, he'd kill her. But would he do it in the car? While they were still moving? Or would he pull over first? If he did, she might have some kind of chance at survival.

She still felt dazed from the blow and at the same time terrified. She wondered how clearly she was actually thinking.

Carson lifted the gun and grinned. "Time's up, Beth!"

Her fingers scrambled to grab the cell phone. She tossed it out the window.

As he closed the window, she glanced over at Carson. She didn't know where he'd gotten the flexi cuffs from but as they landed in her lap, she reached for them.

"Put them on."

She put one side on and tightened it around her wrist. When she went to slide her other wrist through the other side, he stopped her.

"Not in front. In back."

Shifting forward, she put her hands behind her back and even managed to get her second wrist through the plastic loop. As soon as she did, Carson reached over and tightened it. He checked both twice before seeming satisfied.

She leaned back, her hands now trapped behind her. She'd been frightened up to this point, but now the sense of inevitability took her by the throat. She felt the sharp pressure of her full bladder and for the first time understood how frightened people could lose control.

When her gaze met Carson's this time, he grinned.

She realized he also suddenly looked less edgy. Was that because after disarming her, after getting rid of her phone, after binding her, he finally felt back in control?

Should she try to shake him up somehow? Maybe let him know that they'd been aware of his identity since last night? Or would that only serve to tip him off and make him more cautious? And more likely to panic?

Maybe what she needed to do was start with what he would see as a nonthreatening line of questioning.

"Why me?" she asked.

"What do you mean?"

"Of all the people out there, why call me?"

"It was the way you looked at the camera. As if you weren't afraid of anything. As if your confidence was unshakable."

"And you found that appealing?"

"That and the way you looked. I've had some good times just thinking about you, Beth. About what I was going to do to you. All those things I've wanted to do to other women but couldn't because I had a reputation, a life to protect."

Beth swallowed against the expanding lump of fear in her throat. She was breathing shallow and fast almost before she realized it. Catching herself, she tried to slow it down, tried to force more air into her lungs each time.

Now more than ever, she needed to stay calm. Raping her would take time. Would buy time for her to be found.

And as long as he was raping her, maybe people wouldn't be dying.

How much time did she have? How long before they reached the spot he'd chosen for the rape?

Dwelling on the coming attack wasn't going to help her any. Maybe if she kept him talking, she could learn more things about him… Maybe she'd find something that could help her in some way.

"How did you get Thesing to steal the chemical?"

Carson took his eyes off the road. "I didn't. He came to me. He'd gotten cold feet about the chemical and thought the lab should be forced to destroy what they'd stockpiled. He figured that if he stole some, they'd panic at the very least. But they didn't. He contacted me hoping I'd put him in touch with someone who could bring it to the public attention. He figured once people knew, the lab's hand would be forced."

"So how did Thesing wind up dead?"

"I suggested I had a better way to handle things. I'd sell it to the highest bidder."

"And he wasn't about to go along."

"Harvey?" He snorted. "Hell, no. He was a real Boy Scout."

"So why haven't you sold it? I would think it would be worth a large fortune to the right people."

He looked over at her. "You can't spend money where we're both headed."

Chapter Twenty-One

Mark was ankle deep in mud by the time he could grab Beth's cell phone out of the ditch bordering the Florida Turnpike.

After negotiating the slick incline, he flung the phone into the backseat of the SUV and then turned as a semi rig roared past.

Carson seemed to be headed north, but he would have had numerous opportunities to switch cars so there was no way to be even certain what type of vehicle he was driving now. It wasn't the BMW registered to him, though. That one was still safely parked in Carson's garage.

And what about the MX141? Had Carson had it with him when he'd taken Beth this morning? Or was that where he was headed now? To retrieve the chemical?

And once he did, what then? Where was he planning to use it? And what were his plans for Beth?

As he jumped back into the SUV, his cell phone rang. This time the voice belonged to Jenny Springer. "Beth's credit card is being used at a gas station just north of YeeHaw Junction. Highway patrol has been alerted and they're on the way."

Tires spun, the back end of the SUV fishtailing as it

lunged back onto the roadway. YeeHaw Junction was only a few miles ahead. Five or seven at most.

Mark watched in the rearview mirror as the white pickup changed lanes to avoid hitting him. "Are they aware of what Carson may have onboard?"

"They've been told about the chemical."

"How far is the nearest Hazmat Response Unit?" Mark asked.

"Miami," Jenny said. "I'll contact them now."

"Any idea what kind of car they're in?"

"A black Taurus."

"Tell Highway Patrol to stay back. We need to find a way to limit casualties here."

He had to find a way to save Beth.

But what if she was already dead? What if after throwing away her phone, Carson had already killed her, thrown her away, too?

Mark jerked a hand through his hair. He couldn't start thinking like that. She was smart. Resourceful. Tenacious. If any woman could survive Carson, she could.

Mark glanced down at the assault rifle on the passenger seat. And she would know that he was coming for her.

Or would she?

Maybe she hadn't understood what sending her to safety had meant. That he couldn't handle the idea of anything happening to her. That he had put her safety so far above everyone else's that it made a mockery of the oath he'd taken.

Catching sight of the black Taurus just ahead, Mark closed in cautiously, getting only close enough to see that there was a passenger in the car before backing off. The Taurus was sticking to the speed limit and to the right-hand lane. Carson was trying to play it safe. He couldn't afford to be stopped. Not with Beth in the car.

As Mark followed just far enough behind that Carson wouldn't spot him, he tried to determine the best way to take down Carson. The safest way to rescue Beth while putting as few people as possible at risk.

As they continued to travel north, other agents joined the procession, some ahead of Carson and others behind Mark. So far Carson still hadn't done anything that would indicate he knew he was being followed.

He'd moved into the center lane now, but still stayed reasonably close to the posted speed.

And then suddenly, just south of Orlando, Carson swerved across the right lane, nearly colliding with a delivery truck as he took the exit ramp at the last second, forcing Mark and the others to do the same.

Now that they'd been made, it was time to end things. They couldn't afford to hold off any longer. They had to take down Carson fast and hard. Before he had a chance to use the MX141.

But Mark couldn't block out that it was Beth sitting beside Carson right now.

Acceptable casualties.

For every other officer involved in the takedown, she was just that. They couldn't worry about one life when there was a far greater number hanging in the balance.

But if you loved that one person…

Mark shot around the black Taurus, cutting him off as other agents raced to box him in on all sides. The road was a rural two-lane.

As the cars in front of Carson slowed, he was forced to, as well. He tried to muscle the car to his left out of the way, but the midsize vehicle he was in didn't have enough mass to accomplish it.

As soon as the Taurus came to a stop, the passenger door was pushed open and Carson shoved Beth out first, keeping her in front of him and the open door still at his back. He was wearing body armor over his clothing. He tossed a small navy-blue duffel on the ground at their feet.

Beth's hands appeared to be bound behind her, otherwise she seemed to be in reasonably good shape.

Carson reached back and grabbed something that had been on the passenger seat. It wasn't the assault rifle that Mark expected, it was a shotgun.

Instead of pointing it toward them, Carson seemed to aim it at the duffel. Why? Because the bag held the chemical? Because he'd developed a new method of dispersal that he was about to try out?

"If you want to live, you'll back off," Carson yelled.

Mark couldn't take his eyes off Beth's face. She'd survived this long because she was smart. She'd known how to handle Carson.

"Do what you have to, Mark," she yelled. "Kill him here and now."

Mark couldn't though.

Everything seemed to go briefly silent. Even the breeze that sifted by. The grasses along the road swayed gracefully beneath a painfully blue sky. Sunlight reflected off the road sign just visible behind Carson and Beth. Seeing it, Mark knew what Carson's target had been. One of the area's many theme parks.

"Do the right thing," Beth yelled, "before more people get hurt."

She suddenly threw her body backward, slamming the

back of her skull into Carson's chin and then dropping to the ground in one fluid motion. Trusting him with her life.

Mark took the shot, delivering a quick double-tap. Everything was still moving in slow motion, allowing him to really see, to dissect each second. To live in it. To feel the relief as Beth looked up and smiled at him. And then to feel the terror as Carson's shotgun went off. The duffel bag exploded, a geyser of fluid spraying anything within range. Carson staggered a few feet before going down.

Beth went into convulsions, her body jerking as if she was hooked up to a thousand volts.

Throwing down the assault rifle, Mark rushed forward.

Several agents tried to stop him, but he broke free.

Grabbing her with his bare hands, he dragged her away from the debris.

He barely had time to uncap the autoinjector and to plunge it into her thigh muscle before his own body started to feel the effects of the nerve agent.

Pulling the cap off the second injector, he plunged it into his own thigh.

Chapter Twenty-Two

Hours later when he first started coming around, Mark didn't know where he was or what had happened to him. Why his head hurt and why his muscles continued to contract painfully.

He tried to move, but he couldn't, and because it was easier, he allowed himself to sink into the warm nothingness again.

The next time he floated to consciousness, he realized that he was in a darkened hospital room. He could hear the rhythmic beep of a monitor somewhere behind him, the soft hiss of the oxygen mask. The sounds beyond the closed doors that suggested, despite the gloom in the room, that it was daytime.

As he came around a bit more, he finally remembered what had happened. The reason he was in a hospital bed. His gut twisted as memories flooded his brain.

Beth collapsing onto the pavement.

Hands holding him back as he tried to reach her.

The moment he'd broken free.

Her body convulsing as he dragged her away.

And then…and then nothing.

He clenched his eyes shut at the sudden pain of realization ripping through him.

Beth?

The door opened, harsh light stabbing his eyes briefly before it dropped closed behind whoever had entered. He tried to turn his head but couldn't seem to make his body work.

The nurse leaned over him. "They've given you medications to slow muscle contractions. You'll be able to move normally by tomorrow."

"Beth?" he managed to get out but even to his own ears it sounded more like a soft exhale than a name.

The nurse pulled the blanket up, adjusted the position of the oxygen line and checked the IVs.

As she was preparing to leave, her hand brushed across his and he managed to close his fingers on hers.

She looked down, her expression startled but kind.

"Beth?" He knew he was crying but didn't care.

Her expression softened. Because he couldn't, she slowly turned his head for him.

"She's right there."

"How?"

"She'll be fine."

Epilogue

Six Weeks Later

Beth took the last turn up the steep gravel drive, pulling in behind the silver Explorer. Because of the Christmas trip to Sanibel, Florida, and the fitness evaluation she'd had to undergo as a formality, it had been nearly three weeks since she'd seen Mark at Larson's funeral. Even though they'd talked often on the phone, she'd missed him even more than she'd expected.

But had he missed her?

Stalling now, she took a few moments to check out the quaint two-story cabin surrounded by tall pine trees. The snow that had fallen overnight clung not just to the front of the structure but to the branches of the trees, too. With no other homes in sight, the idyllic scene almost resembled a Christmas card.

Still fighting a mixture of excitement and apprehension, she climbed out. The air was unbelievably frigid, the kind of dry cold that seemed to burn the lungs. For several seconds, she absorbed the utter silence, and then closed the door behind her.

She started to retrieve her suitcase from the backseat, but then didn't. This wasn't just the first time she'd been invited up here, it was also the first time she was to meet Gracie and Addison.

What if they didn't like her?

Mark opened the front door even before she reached it. Her heart turned over and then raced as he smiled at her.

"Sorry I couldn't get here sooner," she said nervously. "I had to wait on the carpenter. He's going to start the remodeling in the morning." Once she'd taken down the wall between the kitchen and the breakfast room, she'd decided to indulge in a new kitchen.

"You're right on time. I was just putting the spaghetti on." He closed the door behind her. "How are you in the kitchen?"

"Spaghetti I can handle."

Grinning, he pulled her into his arms. "What about me? Can you handle me?"

She twisted her fingers into his shirt collar and dragged his mouth down until it was a whisper from hers. "Depends on what kind of handling you're interested in."

Sensing that they were no longer alone, she pulled back awkwardly. Mark's two daughters stood near the hall entrance. As Beth smiled, the one she assumed because of her size was Addison, reached for her sister's hand. Evidently, Beth wasn't the only one who was nervous.

"Gracie, Addison. I'd like you to meet Beth."

They both approached, offering their small hands for her to shake, but neither of them said anything.

Reaching into her coat pocket, Beth produced two wrapped jewelry boxes. She was still uncomfortably aware that they might see the gifts as an attempt to bribe them into liking her. And maybe it was just a little bit.

She knelt down. "I went to Florida over the holidays," she said uncertainly as she handed out the presents.

Even as Addison ripped away the paper, Gracie stood unmoving.

Addison's small fingers picked up the delicate silver bracelet with a dolphin charm.

"Your dad told me that last summer when you went to Florida, you and Gracie and your mom got to swim with the dolphins."

Perhaps only because she knew she had to, Gracie slowly peeled open her gift and, like Addison, picked up the bracelet.

"What do you say, girls?" Mark asked.

Both Gracie and Addison chimed in with a thank-you, but Addison stepped forward, offering a brief hug that Beth hadn't been prepared for.

"You're both welcome."

Mark motioned with his head. "Why don't you girls go play another game of checkers while Beth and I finish dinner?"

Watching them leave, Beth knew she'd been expecting too much. She'd been eager to meet Mark's daughters and had been anxious that like her, but she couldn't expect them to share those sentiments.

Mark wrapped her hand in his. "Come on. You can tell me all the news while I boil pasta."

The kitchen smelled divine. Homey. Mark turned up the burner beneath the pot and then handed her a glass of red wine, steering her to a bar stool. "Sit. Relax."

"I thought you wanted help."

"No. I just wanted to know if you can cook. For future reference." He picked up a carrot, scraping it clean and then slicing it expertly. "So how's your new boss?"

"Tom? He's doing fine." When Bill Monroe was suddenly transferred to Idaho, Tom Weston had been promoted to supervisory special agent.

She took a quick sip. "In fact on the way up here today, I learned that I've been completely cleared, that I'll be returning to full duties after the holidays." She'd thought it would bother her that after everything Monroe had done to her, the only punishment he'd received was a transfer. But it didn't.

He dumped the noodles into the strainer. "Where's your luggage?"

"I left it in the car for now."

"In case you have to make a fast escape?"

"I just wasn't sure… You have the girls this weekend. I thought maybe it wouldn't be wise…"

He crossed to where she sat and pulled her into his arms. "You're the first woman I've invited up here since the divorce. And the first one I've introduced to them. And there's a reason that both of those things are true, Beth."

She knew what he was trying to say. That what he felt for her wasn't casual. She'd known for weeks now that she was in love with him, but it was scary being that way alone.

Cradling her face between his warm hands, he lowered his lips. "What I'm trying to say is I love you." He kissed her slowly and completely. "And I'm hoping that you feel the same way about me."

Emotion welled up inside her as she met his gaze. "I do."

"Enough to say those same two words in front of a minister?"

She wanted to throw herself into his arms, but something kept her from doing it.

"Marry me, Beth."

"What about the girls? What if they don't like me?"

"Maybe they won't. Maybe they'll love you instead." He straightened. "I know it's a package deal. And I know we've never talked about how you feel about children, or about babies. If you don't want to have children of your own, I understand—"

"But I do. And I want to have them with you."

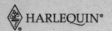

the DEVIL'S footprints

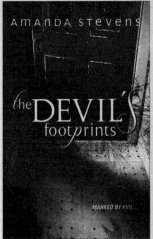

AMANDA STEVENS

the DEVIL'S footprints

MARKED BY EVIL...

Don't miss
the latest thriller from

AMANDA STEVENS

On sale March 2008!

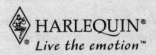

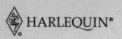
#1047 IN NAME ONLY? by Patricia Rosemoor
The McKenna Legacy
This wasn't Michael Eagan's first high-profile murder case—but it *was* his first McKenna. He'll have to be a good man to charm Flanna, and live dangerously to keep her alive.

#1048 MYSTERIOUS MILLIONAIRE by Cassie Miles
Wealthy adventurer Dylan Crawford is a man of many secrets. So when Elle Norton goes undercover on his estate to investigate a family death, what she discovers about the man is more revealing than she expected.

#1049 WYOMING MANHUNT by Ann Voss Peterson
Thriller
Riding horseback through the Wyoming wilderness was supposed to be the trip of a lifetime for Shanna Clarke—instead she found herself running for her life. Now only rancher Jace Lantry can help her find justice—and exact revenge.

#1050 THE HORSEMAN'S SON by Delores Fossen
Five-Alarm Babies
Collena Drake thought she'd never see her son again after he was stolen at birth. But she found him, in the care of Dylan Greer, a wealthy Texas horse breeder with a dark past. Despite their differences, the two would have to work together to uncover an illegal adoption ring to build their new family.

#1051 AVENGING ANGEL by Alice Sharpe
Elle Medina was the sole survivor of a brutal slaying—and sought to bring down the crime boss that set it off. Undercover DEA agent Pete Waters was tasked with keeping that man alive. At cross purposes, neither knew mercy—in love or death.

#1052 TEXAS-SIZED SECRETS by Elle James
Cattle rustlers, ranch foreclosure and pregnancy were all Texas-sized problems that even Mona Grainger wasn't stubborn enough to think she could handle alone. Enter Reed Bryson, who could ride, rope, kiss… and certainly handle a gun.